The TREASURE TREE

by father & daughter

BRUCE & VERNAE EWING

HIGH BRIDGE BOOKS

HOUSTON

The Treasure Tree

by Bruce Ewing & Vernae Ewing

Copyright © 2015 by Bruce Ewing & Vernae Ewing
All rights reserved.

Printed in the United States of America
ISBN (Paperback): 978-1-940024-60-8
ISBN (eBook): 978-1-940024-61-5

High Bridge Books titles may be purchased in bulk for educational, business, fundraising, or sales promotional use. For information please contact High Bridge Books via www.HighBridgeBooks.com/contact.

Published in Houston, Texas by High Bridge Books

To God be the glory.

*This book is dedicated to
our family and friends who serve the
kingdom of God with steadfast love.*

Blessings on you.

CONTENTS

CHARACTERS

Joel: king of the Growers, seer, prophet, watchman

Julia: wife of Joel, mother of Trobus

Trobus: king of the Growers, seer, prophet, watchman, husband of Emma, father of Jedidiah and Beverly

Beverly: sister of Jedidiah, daughter of Trobus and Emma

Jedidiah: king of the Growers, seer, prophet, son of Trobus and Emma, father of Heather

Heather: wife of Steven, mother of Patience

Pricilla: wife of Jedidiah, mother of Heather

Matt: son of Jeremy and Frances Loman

Patience: wife of Matt, daughter of Steven and Heather, granddaughter of Jedidiah

Paul Jackson: son of Jack and Junia Jackson

Jack: father of Jackson, husband of Junia

Junia: mother of Jackson, wife of Jack

Steven Marwari: husband of Heather and father of Patience

Peter and Mary: Steven's parents, Patience's grandparents

Mary: wife of Peter, mother of Steven

"Do not store up for yourselves treasures on earth,
where moth and rust destroy,
and where thieves break in and steal."

—*Matthew 6:19*

Chapter 1

THE GROWERS AND
THE CITY DWELLERS

It was a world of war, corruption, and greed. A place filled with City Dwellers whose only thoughts were evil. After years of living like dogs, it was hard to change, and there was no leader among them strong enough to pull them out of the living hell they had made for themselves. The people were driven by every kind of immoral, wicked desire. Every king in the land fought each other until nothing was left. Death and destruction brought famine and disease. People reverted to the lowest level of instinct. Some even killed and consumed their own children.

The three remaining kings of the City Dwellers formed an alliance in one last attempt to survive, hoping to avoid more of the inevitable coming doom of starvation and death. City Dwellers thought, by taking the stored provisions collected by the people called Growers, they would prolong their own lives.

The Growers were not only farmers but people of kindness and great faith. They were led by a seer named Joel, a benevolent man who feared God and loved people. His clothes were made of common leather and camel's hair. He was well over 200 years old, but no one could tell it by his appearance. He was gray haired and had a smooth face unlike most his age. He stood head and shoulders above most men and had the strength of an ox.

Although Julia his wife had departed to be with Jesus, his love for people kept him fit for the work that the Lord had given him to do. His purpose was to provide food for all the nations. His protest against the wars had gone unheeded. Consequently, the wars devastated the land so much that very little food could be produced. Storage bins under the Growers' care held the last remaining food, and all the kings of the land wanted it.

Joel was also a king, the King of the Growers, but without a visible crown. He understood how emotional and unpredictable people could be. For years, he had encountered the malevolent will and attitude of the City Dwellers. He easily could have won the wars between the kings, but war was not his way. The other kings of the land hated him, but they also respected who he was. Without a doubt, they all feared his God and knew that the words he spoke were true. Nonetheless, they still chose evil over life.

Joel made it known to all that he had no desire to kill his enemy. As a seer and watchman, Joel was charged by the Lord to protect his people. His only recourse to avoid war was to get the Growers to safety. To do that, he would have to take them to the

Land of the West. However, leaving was a huge task that called for desperate measures.

In a dream years before the wars commenced, Joel saw the coming destruction. His attempt to warn the Kings of the City Dwellers was futile.

Joel also had seen the only way of escape for the Growers was by building enormous ships. He had these ships built secretly with oversized sails that would enable them to move fast and swift in the water. He built 50 ships. Each ship could carry 400 people, providing a way of escape for 20,000 people plus their cargo. He then hid them behind the forest next to the ocean, behind mountainous rocks where they could not be seen.

The plan was made, the people were set to go, and the time had come.

*****

The treaty between the Growers and the City Dwellers had long been severed. The great Black Forest between the Dwellers and the Growers served as a natural boundary. As long as the City Dwellers left Joel and his people to themselves, food and provisions were supplied for all the kingdoms.

Years passed swiftly, but time did not change the hatred the City Dwellers held against the Growers. Many of the Growers were fed-up far beyond their tolerance for the way they were being treated by the nations around them. How could a people filled with kindness be hated by those who depended on their generosity for survival? And yet, that was how things were.

If it was not for the fear of the Black Forest, the City Dwellers would have killed and taken everything from the Growers long ago. The fear of the forest that held the Dwellers back was thick and black, hauntingly eerie, and it wrapped around a human body like a blanket. It was the kind that could suffocate or be touched. It was the Lord's doing.

*****

As destiny would have it, on the day Joel commanded his people to ready themselves to leave, a great star fell from the sky. The impact was so great that it shook every kingdom in the East. The star landed in the middle of the Black Forest. Trees caught fire and crashed to the ground while surrounding mountains shook, throwing pieces of falling rocks in all directions.

The Seer told his son, Trobus, to board all the people on the ships and be ready to set sail before sunrise even if he failed to return. The warrior in Trobus wanted to stand and, for once, do what should have been done years ago: destroy the evil nations around them and let peace rule in the place of chaos. Reluctantly, Trobus obeyed. It was hard to carry out an order that could have left him fatherless. One parent gone and the possibility of losing the other was unthinkable. Trobus pressed his father to let him go instead. He was his father's match in every way; at least, he thought so. He even matched his father's strength, wisdom, and stature, but the king's word was law not even a son could disobey. He was ashamed for challenging his father and heartbroken over the decision that was made. Nevertheless, he carried out his father's orders. He quickly gathered his commanders of thousands, hundreds, and fifties—including household leaders—and instructed them to prepare to sail before dawn.

For the first time, light invaded the Black Forest when the brilliant star crashed to the earth. It gave off multiple colors, and the heat of it melted everything around. Patches of darkness dissipated as fire consumed underbrush surrounding trees. Now was the time for the City Dwellers to find the Growers. Now was the time to strike and take what they wanted. Banding themselves together, the City Dweller's kings raced on horseback and in chariots toward the fallen star, hoping the fire and light would last long enough for them to locate the Growers' hiding place.

*****

Joel took four warriors with him and wasted no time in reaching the star. He had seen the star in a vision and knew that it was vital to the Growers' wellbeing. He knew that it was the will of the

Lord for the star to be with the Growers, and he was not about to let it fall into the hands of devil worshipers.

When Joel arrived, he and the four men hurried down into the crater. There before them laid a smoldering sphere the size of a honey melon, still giving off multiple beautiful colors unlike any they had ever seen. They could hear the trampling of many feet coming through the forest preceded by war cries and angry voices. The intruders had to leave their horses and chariots because the forest was too thick for them to pass through. Joel ordered the men to open the silver box he had provided for the treasure. To their amazement, the sphere rose up on its own and entered the box. He then ordered the men to rush it back to the ships and deliver it into the hands of his son, Trobus.

"What of you, my lord? We cannot go back without you." All four men felt the same, but the king would not have it. He ordered them to return with the precious treasure and assured them that he would join them later.

The City Dwellers arrived in time to see Joel as he cleared the top of the crater. They saw no one else. The four men who had been with Joel found themselves on the beach just below Trobus' ship. How they got there so fast was a mystery to them. Trobus called them aboard as he glanced at the sundial to determine the time. The men immediately put the box into Trobus' hand, and he gave it to Emma, his wife.

"Where are we going, Father?" asked the young Jedidiah.

"To a place called Truevine, Son. A place in the West, free of war."

"But where is Grandfather?" asked the concerned Jedidiah.

"He is in the Lord's hand and will join us soon," said Trobus, clinging to hope and trusting his faith.

Jedidiah was saddened by what he heard. Looking into the eyes of his father and feeling the hand of his mother on his shoulder, he bowed his head. He had heard that kind of talk before. Sometimes, it was true. Other times, it turned out completely different. He stood between his mother and his little sister, Beverly. Thank God Beverly was still too young to understand what was going on. Holding back tears that might otherwise have upset her, he took her hand and held it. Emma placed her hand on Jedidiah's head and softly kissed it. He heard his mother praying, something she often did that always made him feel better.

The seer, Joel, diligently tried to persuade the City Dwellers to forsake their evil intent, but it was a futile effort. The end times of the City Dwellers had come. The light from the fire in the forest had drawn the kings and the majority of their armies to the place where Joel stood. Joel warned them to leave while they could, but obstinate pride prevented them from listening. The city kings demanded to have the object that had fallen from the sky. Joel explained that the sphere was a gift from God to the Growers and that he had no intention of relinquishing it to them.

Blind rage took over. Rocks, swords, and arrows were hurled at the old seer, but none harmed him. He pointed his staff at those who had assaulted him. He then turned and shook the dust off his feet and headed back to the ships. The City Dwellers and their kings set out to follow, but as soon as they took steps toward Joel, roots and vines from the forest floor took hold of them. With every movement they made, the vines held them tighter, pulling them down into the ground. It was terrifying. All those who entered the forest never came out. The last thing they saw was the King of the Growers walking away, a king who wore no crown. Seconds later, he vanished from their sight as they vanished beneath the earth.

Trobus stood on the bow of his ship, watching in desperation for his father to return. It wasn't long before he saw a familiar form coming toward him with staff in hand. Trobus felt tension leave his body and normal breathing resume. "Thank you, God, for helping my father," he said as he wrapped his arms around Emma and their children.

Jedidiah held his sister's hand tighter as they all watched Joel board the ship. Joel opened his arms as his children ran to embrace him as if for the first time. The heartbreaking irony of it all was that it would be their last. The greeting was short-lived, and the joyful experience suddenly waned into sorrow. It seemed that the old seer had other plans.

Many City Dwellers had died from the way they had chosen to live. Many were still alive and without hope. Joel had a burden for these lost people. He felt the call of God in his heart to stay with the City Dwellers. If there was a chance of him turning even one person from the oncoming destruction, he wanted that chance.

When he looked into the eyes of his father, Trobus knew that it would be of no use trying to talk him out of it. They embraced again, and Joel kissed his children and blessed his people. He warned them to love God and each other lest what happened to the City Dwellers would happen to them.

Before sailing westward toward the City Dwellers, he gave his staff to Trobus and then reached into a pocket that seemed to appear in his robe when he reached into it. Out came a beautiful, jeweled crown. He placed it on Trobus' head and kissed him. After a long embrace and tears, the last grandchild let go of his robe.

Joel then made a spectacle of himself by jumping from the bow of the ship into the water below. A great cry went out from the onlookers as they watched their leader plummet to the await-ing death below. Just before he hit the ground, a giant water spout in the form of a hand caught him and held him up for all to see. The old seer laughed and pointed his finger at them all. The sad-ness left, and laughter filled the air. The Growers had never seen anything like it. It was God's gift to them, all just to assure them that those who put their trust in God will be just fine. Joel waved goodbye as the water spout placed him gently on the shore below.

As the sails opened and the wind filled them, the most wonderful thing happened. All 50 of the ships took off as if they were flying, and when they looked down at the water and found themselves surrounded by clouds, they knew indeed that they were flying. What would have taken a year by water took only three days by airships. It was a most wonderful experience for the Growers. Never had they seen or enjoyed such pleasure. They were sure nothing would ever be more exhilarating than flying through the sky on clouds.

*****

When Truevine appeared below them, it was like landing in the Garden of Eden. Each family was given a parcel of land to own and cultivate according to their ability. Life was amazing, and as long as the Growers continued to love God and each other, they had no difficulty living a wonderful life.

Time passed, and so did Joel and his son, Trobus. Emma spent her last days enjoying her children, grandchildren, and great-grandchildren. Jedidiah was the delight of her heart, and she gave her blessings to him just as his father, Trobus, had given him wisdom for his time to serve. Emma lived to see Jedidiah marry the wife of his youth, a young girl named Pricilla. She was attractive but not a stunning beauty. Her smile, however, was captivating. At age 10, she decided that Jedidiah was the one she was going to marry. Their friendship over the years proved her right. A daughter was born to them, Heather, who was the apple of her father's eye. It seemed that the gift of Queen Esther's beauty was given to the daughters of Seers, for there was none more beautiful than Heather. Her golden hair sparkled like the sun, and her green eyes set her apart from those in Jedidiah's ancestral line. The man she chose for her husband was strong and courageous, a man of few words who worked hard and served God.

As the years passed, the new land brought with it wealth and prosperity. Unfortunately, over time, many of the Growers forsook the way of the Lord that had been taught continuously by every Seer and Watchman. From the noble Joel to the day Jedidiah took over as Seer, there had been those among the Growers who had not embraced the way of Jesus. The land, Truevine, still produced much, but it seemed that the more it produced, the more the people lost sight of who provided for them.

*****

The day finally came when Jedidiah took his rightful place as King of the Growers and gave his life to serving them. Jedidiah chose to live his life serving others, and he did it in a most unusual way.

On the first day of his reign, a great famine came over the land of Truevine. It lasted for three years. It took that long before the Growers came to their senses to seek the Lord and obey the king. Most of the people returned to serving God and each other, but there remained a few whose greed and rebellion kept them from a life of contentment. That is why the Lord charged Jedidiah with the command to provide for the people in a new way.

In years to come, during certain seasons, famine would come to remind the people that it was the Lord who provided for them. The Lord gave Jedidiah authority over the land to produce food and provision for every village that humbled itself to ask for help. Like his fathers before him, Jedidiah had a benevolent heart and was bent on standing firm for righteousness. This story is about how he lived to please God, his family, and his people.

Chapter 2

TWO VISITORS

There once was an old man who lived in the wilderness of a place called Truevine. He had hundreds of fields in which he planted enough food to feed many villages. One day, as he was sitting under a great tree, two men approached him. The first man was youthful with a hairless, boyish face and piercing green eyes. His hair was dark brown with a natural part on the left. He displayed a medium-sized, lanky body frame that could have used a few extra pounds in the right places.

The second man was tall and muscular with brown eyes, blonde hair, and a sculptured face. Women found him attractive, and he was used to being center of attention. They traveled from the village, Columbidae, to speak with him because they had heard he was a wise and noble man. They also had heard that he had read every book in the world and knew many languages. There was not a map or manuscript he could not decipher or understand. Two other qualities he displayed were the ability to read signs and wonders in celestial bodies as well as the human heart with accuracy.

The young men were not the first ones to seek out the old man. There had been many visitors who traveled to see him for various reasons, but very few had gotten what they desired. It was believed by the village people that the wise man also knew where buried treasure could be found. If anyone could answer his questions and perform the task the old man asked of them, at the completion of the task, he would reward them with a box filled with precious treasure.

As the young men approached the large tree under which the old man rested, they stopped dead in their tracks. A frightening scene occurred right before their eyes. The large tree under which the old man sat raised its limbs and signaled for the two men to stop. Astounded at what they saw, they fell down in fear, for no one had ever seen a tree that could raise its limbs like human arms or point its branches like fingers.

The old man stood and approached the bowing men and chuckled a little as he touched them with his staff. Their fear seem to dissipate, and they were able to stand again without feeling faint.

"What are you doing here?" the old man asked.

"We have come to seek wisdom," said one of the young men.

"And treasure," said the other.

"So you have come to receive something... have you?" replied the old man.

"Yes, Sir," they both replied, still bowing to the ground.

"And what have you brought to give in place of receiving?"

"We were not aware that we had to bring something," said the second man.

"But we will be willing to give anything we have if we are allowed to return home to fetch it," said the first man.

They both raised their heads for a glimpse of the speaker, but he was shrouded in mystery that hid his true form.

"That will not be necessary. What you have with you will be sufficient.

"We have nothing," said the first man.

"Oh, but you have more than you think," replied the old man.

So the two men found themselves rising and following the old man to the tree. As they walked, the old man said under his breath but loud enough for them to hear, "You will get more of a blessing when you give than when you receive."

When they reached the tree, the old man asked them to sit and have tea with him. "I will pour you a cup of tea," said the old man politely.

"Tea? Is that all you have to drink?" asked the second man.

"I think you will find that the tea will satisfy your thirst... whatever it is."

So the second man took a cup and found that it was as the old man had said. In his cup was the strong taste of wine, and he greedily drank it down. After about the third cup, he offered his friend an opportunity to have some of the finest wine he had ever tasted.

His friend declined. "I am pledged to abstain from strong drinks and wines until I reach my appointed time," said the first man.

"What appointed time?" asked the second man.

"The time when I celebrate with thanksgiving what I have received in life on my twenty-first birthday."

"Why wait until then when you can have some now?" replied his friend.

The first man said nothing.

"And how long do you have to wait for your twenty-first birthday?" asked the old man.

"I still have a year, and it seems like it will never get here."

Hardy laughter came from the old man's chest as he shook his head in puzzlement. "That is the problem with young people today. Always in a hurry for time to pass or to go someplace, and when they finally arrive, they have no idea why they were in such a hurry to get there."

"I suppose you are right, Sir, but it still feels good in knowing that the day is not far off."

The old man watched his two guests for a while and then asked them for their names. "Tell me your names, young Men. What are you called?"

The first man sleepily stood, stretched out his arms, and allowed a big yawn and smile to crescent across his face. "I am called Matthew, Matthew Loman, but my friends call me Matt."

With a warm smile, the old man said, "I am pleased to meet you, Matt. And you, my Friend, what are you called?"

The second man started to stand as well, but too much wine tea had made him off-balance, so he remained seated. "I am Paul Jackson, and my friends call me Jackson." he laughed sarcastically.

"Well, Jackson, it is good to meet you as well. I am called, Jedidiah."

"Tell me why you came to see me."

Clearing his throat, Matt said, "Well, Sir, there is a famine in the land, and I heard you could help us. So far, hundreds have died, and the epidemic grows daily. Without proper food and nourishment, I'm afraid that not only famine but sickness and disease will soon overtake us. When my mother told me there was a wise man who could possibly help, well, I jumped at the opportunity. Jackson and I grew up in the same village, and sometimes, we spend time with each other. It just so happens that he was at my house when my mother and I were discussing the matter. We knew that, unless something happened soon, the whole land would lay in waste. My father and other men in our village are working diligently, trying to provide some relief for the families. I believed my mother when she told me of you. She said that, years ago, famine struck our village, and it was miraculously saved from starvation because of your help. Now that the threat of starvation is back, we wanted to see if you would help us again. My friend, Jackson, decided to come along."

As they continued to talk about why they came, the time passed so rapidly that night soon overtook them.

"Well," said the old man, "It looks like you will be spending the night with me."

"Spend the night? You have no shelter out here. Where do you suggest we sleep? On the ground?" asked Jackson.

"If you like," said the old man.

"The ground will be fine, Sir. It's not like we haven't slept on the ground before. We will be content to sleep wherever you suggest," said Matt, giving Jackson a disapproving look.

"You may sleep on the ground or under my tree if you wish, but if you like, you can stay in my home. I have more than enough room."

"Your home? Where is your home?" inquired Jackson.

"Why, it is right behind me, young Man. Can't you see it?"

Neither of the men could see the house because only those who truly sought wisdom and had faith were allowed to see what others would never see.

"I don't see a house," said Matt.

"Me, neither," repeated Jackson.

"That is because your senses are dull, and your faith is weak. What you do not see is there, so look again, and believe."

Right before their eyes, the large tree took the shape of a house with a window on each side and a large, double door in the middle. Over each window was a sky blue overhang that shaded the windows from direct sun. A cat rested on the window sill of one window, and a family of sparrows in their nest did the same on the other window sill. It was strange that birds would live so close to a cat and not be eaten. What the young men failed to understand was everything that lived under or in the tree lived in perfect harmony.

The tree that had become a house didn't appear very big on the outside, but it looked like it could accommodate at least the three of them comfortably. The old man waved his hand in front of the door, and it opened immediately. As they stepped inside, the door closed as fast as it had opened as if not to let anything else in or to prevent anything from getting out.

Once inside, the young men got the surprise of their lives. The place was extraordinarily large. No one would have imagined that such a place could have existed inside a tree. Matt and Jackson looked in disbelief at the size of the place. It was the greatest house they had ever seen. Actually, it was more like a castle or grand mansion with a grand hall that extended 300 yards wide, 100 yards high, and a half mile long. The hall ceiling hung with rows of grand chandeliers, each having hundreds of perfectly shaped crystals hanging down. A large diamond was in the center of each chandelier. On the walls were paintings of what looked like ordinary people. They couldn't really tell because of the hazy mist that surrounded them.

The wall was covered with thousands of precious stones of every kind. There was one jewel that glowed like the sun so much that it was difficult for anyone to look at it for very long. It was spherical in shape, the size of a small melon, and no jewel in the mansion could matched it. It was kept behind a large door that would periodically open at no scheduled time. The jewel was placed in an open diamond container alone in the center of a large room of the east corridor.

The jewel was called the Sun Stone because it was believed that it came from the sun. The legend said it broke off from the sun, and by the time it came to earth, it had burned down to the size of a 12-inch sphere. Unlike most meteors that turn dull and lose their luster after traveling through earth's atmosphere, the sun stone did not. It was the most beautiful of jewels and the rarest among them all.

Unlike the other jewels which shined all the time, the Sun Stone seemed to shine only at certain times like when the birds sung or sunbeams from the real sun glittered on the mirrors in the hall. It shined brightest in the presence of a faithful and pure heart such as that of the old man, Jedidiah. It was like it had a mind of its own, for at times, it would rise up from the diamond casing and hover in the air. The light from it was so dazzling that it would light up the entire mansion when placed in the right position. The walls inside the rooms and in the halls of the mansion were pure gold inlaid with thousands of jewels. It was an awesome sight to see.

In the great hall on a polished wooden floor laid hand-woven rugs from Persia and other exotic places. They were interlaid with pure gold strips that outlined three cat-like figures that resembled a lion, tiger, and one unknown. The animals on the rugs looked so real, but anyone could tell it was the raised threads in the rugs that made them appear that way.

As the young men walked through the hall, they were amazed at the multitude of rooms. It was generous of the old man to give them a choice of any room to rest themselves. Each room had all the comforts that one could imagine, and there was no re-striction as to what room they could use. There were only two stipulations that Jedidiah required of them. Upon leaving, they could take only one thing with them. They could choose anything in the mansion, large or small, as long as they could carry it out. It could be gold or silver, a diamond or another precious stone with the exception of the Sun Stone. No one was to approach or touch it without the consent of Jedidiah. Other than that, they were free to choose one. The other stipulation was that they must, at all times, be honest and truthful about everything. Of course, Matt and Jackson thought it was very generous of Jedidiah to offer them a gift at all, especially when they didn't have one to give to him. And being truthful shouldn't be any trouble either.

"Come, let us go into the dining room. I'm sure you are hungry by now, and I'll be happy to serve you," Jedidiah said.

Matt and Jackson could not believe the hospitality they were receiving. They were amazed that, throughout dinner and the evening conversation, Jedidiah never stopped serving them. They were treated like kings so much so that Jackson began to act like one. As he looked upon the wealth in the house and observed the grandeur of its essence, his heart coveted all that he saw. He wondered why an old man like Jedidiah should have all the wealth and prestige of a king when he and others like him practically lived in poverty. Jackson felt it wasn't right that this wealth should belong to one man and not be distributed out to the poor and others in need. *Why should one man have it all* was the question in Jackson's mind. No one had a right to have so much even if he did own it.

As they continued to walk, Matt noticed something different about Jackson. He had become unusually quiet and constantly was looking around as if he was looking for someone. When Jackson noticed that Matt was watching, he quickly turned his attention back to listening to what Jedidiah was saying.

"Well, Boys, I am going to my room at the end of the hallway to get some rest. I suggest that you do the same. You'll have a big day tomorrow, and you'll need your rest to accomplish the task I have for you."

"Yes, Sir, I think you are right. I am exhausted, and a good night's sleep on a soft bed is calling my name," said Matt, stretching out his arms and yawning loudly with a squeak in his voice.

"You will find rooms up and down the hall. Feel free to choose any one you desire," said Jedidiah as he turned to leave the room.

"I think I would like to look around a little while longer if you don't mind, Sir," said Jackson.

"Hey, Jackson, aren't you tired? We walked over five days getting here, and now you want to run around?"

"I feel fine. That delicious meal we had really energized me," replied Jackson.

Matt rubbed the back of his neck, trying to make sense out of Jackson's sudden desire to want to go gallivanting around the place. He easily could tour the mansion the next day. He decided to leave the decision with Jackson. As for him, he was going to take advantage of a warm bed. The old man had no objections and allowed Jackson to roam his home for as long as he wanted. However, he did remind him that, tomorrow, they had a long day ahead of them and that, if he didn't get enough sleep, he would be unable to keep up on the journey.

As Jedidiah headed toward the door, he turned to say goodnight and then turned again and walked out the door. Matt had one more question to ask and tried to catch him, but as he reached the door, Jedidiah was nowhere to be found. Matt looked to the left and then to the right. Then, he looked straight ahead, but Jedidiah seemingly vanished. *Where did he go so fast?* Matt asked himself. *And why couldn't we get a good look at his face? Why was he so wrapped up in mystery?* He decided that the questions could wait until morning.

"Hey, Jackson, you want to share this room? There's another bed across the room if you want it."

It was kind of Matt to offer, but Jackson wanted his own room to come and go as he pleased. Sleep was the last thing on Jackson's mind. He had no worries about keeping up with Matt and an old man. After all, the journey couldn't be too far. *It was probably just over the hill or something*, he mused to himself. It wasn't enough to be troubled over. He said goodnight to Matt and went looking through the mansion, scouting out every room. It was astonishing how every room was so different… how each was more marvelous than the next. Before long, Jackson found himself so far down the corridor that he hardly could see the place where he started. It had taken him three hours to reach where he was, and he still had only reached halfway. The wonders he saw would have amazed the most curious of minds. As he walked, he noticed a jeweled clock on the wall. It was later than he thought. He decided it was time to head back to his room. He was more fatigued than he thought he would be.

Walking back proved to be just as exciting. He became even more overwhelmed by what he saw the second time. There was nothing in his life that compared to what he now beheld. All of this inside a tree? Who would have thought that such a thing was possible?

As he continued, he saw a blinding glow from the eastern corridor just ahead. He didn't remember passing it. *Was this the stone the old man had mentioned? Was this the most precious jewel of them all? How could I have not seen it?* he thought. What he saw as he approached took his breath away. He was astonished by the many colors that bounced off the walls and filled every dark corner. It must have been as bright as the sun. It made all the sense in the world why Jedidiah called it the Sun Stone. He thought to himself, *What harm could one look cause?* Oh, if only he could see the Sun Stone, he would be satisfied. Although he remembered that Jedidiah had warned them not to even approach the stone, Jackson ignored the warning and approached anyway. He had to see it.

The room from where the glowing light came was now only a few feet from him. However, once he reached the room and stuck his head in, the glow was gone. On the wall in the room were more of the same jewels he had seen in the great hall. In the middle of the room, surrounded by a diamond casing, was an ordinary round stone, dull and gray in color. In front of the casing below the stone, was an ancient silver box with the inscription written on the front, THE GREATEST TREASURE.

With each step Jackson took toward the Sun Stone, eerie sounds began to come from the box. At least, that's what Jackson thought he heard. The sound was like a low growl as if some animal was in the room with him. He could not see what it was or tell where it was coming from. It sounded like a lion but unlike any he had ever heard. Then, another sound came to his ear. This time, it sounded like the cooing of a baby. Then came the growl again. Then, music. Then, crying. Then, laughter. Then, a roar. It was frightening and confusing. Jackson could feel his heart rushing as the roar became louder in his ear until he was gripped by overwhelming fear. He slowly backed away from the stone, hoping to escape the room before whatever was in it seized him.

Relief rushed over him as he exited the room. He leaned up against the outer wall to regain his composure. Oddly enough, he never saw the beast, but he sure felt the presence of something, and it wasn't good. Immediately, Jackson headed away from the room but couldn't help wondering what was in the box. All he could think of on his way back to the front part of the mansion was the message on the box, THE GREATEST TREASURE. *What could that be*, he wondered. *If it's the greatest treasure ever, then it has to be more valuable than anything in the great house, including the Sun Stone.* His craving for the box grew stronger. Jackson ignored the fact that greed is never satisfied and that want would always pursue more. His head was spinning from all the excitement, and his heart craved all that he had seen. He finally decided that he should head back toward his room. He was still confused but a little less fearful as he walked away from the room.

As Jackson made his way back, plaguing thoughts consumed his mind. *If I take one item from each room, it shouldn't matter to the old man. After all, he did say that I could take one item from a room.* With a cunning smile, Jackson reasoned with himself, *If I visit all of the rooms and take one gift, that would be the same as taking one gift.* It sounded honest enough to Jackson in a devious kind of way, but to a deceptive heart, evil becomes good. He knew that Jedidiah had said specifically that they could only take one thing with them when they left. *Surely, a man of such great wealth did not intend for us to take only one gift,* he kept repeating to himself.

Then, for a moment, it looked like his conscience was getting through to him. Unfortunately, greed quickly silenced that thought and pushed Jackson on to do what was in his heart. Jackson argued with himself as he looked around for something in which to carry his treasure. A bag appeared. Jackson looked at the bag and decided that he could make good use of it. He continued to talk to himself. *I can sure use this bag. Maybe it's a sign that it's okay to take some of the jewels with me.* Jackson had forgotten what Jedidiah had said about *what a person thinks often happens...* just like the tea that turned to strong wine when he imagined it.

Nevertheless, Jackson started collecting jewels and precious stones wherever he saw them, putting them into the bag. He collected them from the wall and from the frames that contained the strange pictures. He was like a kid in a candy store. Everything he wanted and could fit in the bag, he took. Soon, minutes became hours, and time slipped away from him. The bag grew heavy, and he grew exhausted. There was no way he was going to be able to work the following day if he did not get rest.

While Jackson was collecting precious jewels and looking for a place to stash his loot, he thought to himself, *How stupid Matt is for not taking advantage of the opportunity to get rich.*

Matt, however, was enjoying everything around him. He showered and refreshed himself and then proceeded toward his resting room. Feeling refreshed after a long journey, Matt sat on his bed. Looking down slightly, he saw a pair of new pajamas. Puzzled, Matt tightened his robe while looking around the room to see who had left the garments. He mumbled to himself, "Strange… These garments were not here earlier, and I never heard anyone enter this room. Either my hearing has gone bad, or this place is filled with light-footed people." He smiled. Shrugging off the bizarre occurrence, Matt decided to wear the pajamas, thinking perhaps the old man provided the garments. He then knelt and prayed as was his custom. It wasn't long before his eyes closed, and he found himself sleeping peaceably. The old man stood outside Matt's door very pleased. Jedidiah believed Matt would be ready for tomorrow's challenges but was afraid Jackson would be exhausted. Jackson had gathered all he could carry, but he was too far from his room to make it back in time to rest. His mind was taken with all the wonders around him. He was too consumed by greed to be concerned with rest.

The old man wanted Jackson to make the right decision, but the choice had to be his. He prayed that Jackson would come to his senses like his friend, Matt. Jackson, however, had other plans. By the time Jackson had gone through every room and collected the jewels, it was almost morning. Clinching the bag tightly, Jackson proceeded to find a place to stash his loot obscured from intruding eyes. He decided to leave the treasure box for last and would collect it once leaving the mansion.

Chapter 3

THE FIELDS

The old rooster perched himself on the windowsill and crowed as the sun raised its head from behind the mountains. Jackson only had time to hide his loot and lay his head on the pillow for 30 minutes. A knock on the door startled Jackson, and he jumped up out of bed so fast that it made him dizzy. For a moment, confusion swarmed his mind. Unable to recognize where he was, running his hands through his hair, he suddenly remembered he was in the old man's house. He quickly checked behind the bed on the right side of the headboard, relieved to see his loot was still there. He smiled. A firmer knock on the door told Jackson he needed to hurry. Opening the door, Jackson found Matt standing in front of him, bright-eyed and refreshed.

"Jedidiah wants to see us right away," Matt said to Jackson.

"He does, does he? Well, tell him I'm not feeling well, and if it's alright with him, I would like to stay and rest a little more."

Studying Jackson's face, Matt became curious as to why Jackson was acting strange and why he needed more rest. Then, he saw that Jackson had on the same clothes from the day before. "Did you go to bed last night?" Matt asked, knowing very well that he hadn't because he was wearing the same clothes. Matt wanted to see if Jackson was going to be honest or tell a lie. Jackson decided to say nothing to Matt, hoping he would just go away. "What were you doing all night?" asked Matt.

"Minding my own business... like you should be doing," Jackson replied. Irritated at Matt's question, he pushed past him on his way out. Matt followed, and they both arrived in the kitchen where the old man had asked them to meet him. Jedidiah had a big breakfast prepared with fruit, pastries, ham, eggs, and fish along with a variety of nuts and breads. He poured glasses of creamy cold milk with strawberries and freshly squeezed orange juice. The sweet fragrance of a special tea was in the air.

"Are you ready to eat?" asked Jedidiah.

"I'll say," said Matt, giving Jedidiah a hardy hug and friendly smile.

Jackson said good morning, but there was something in his voice that told Jedidiah that all was not well.

"Is there something wrong, Jackson? Did you get enough rest last night?" asked Jedidiah.

"Yes, and now that you've asked, Matt is my problem." Matt and Jedidiah both looked at Jackson, concerned about his outburst.

"No matter where I go with him, he always kisses up to the person in charge. He's always trying to get an advantage to make himself look good, and I'm sick of it." Jackson had not meant to say so much, but the cat was out of the bag, and words could not be taken back.

"I didn't know you felt that way, Jackson. It was never my intention to come across like that," said Matt.

"There you go again, trying to make me look like the bad guy in front of the old man."

"Is that so?" interjected Jedidiah.

Jackson settled his mind for a moment in order to smooth things over. "I'm still a little tired," he said, exhaling deeply. "I'll be okay." He then sat down at the table.

The old man smiled and spoke to Jackson with gentleness in his voice. "I think you have Matt wrong, Jackson. You have mistaken Matt's kindness for deceitfulness. I can tell when people are honest and when they are not. A good breakfast always makes me feel better, and after you eat something, I'm sure you will feel refreshed and ready to go," chimed Jedidiah.

Jackson said nothing else for the moment, and they all sat down to eat as Jedidiah gave thanks to God for the food.

The old man told them about the trip he had planned for them and also about the work they were to perform in order to receive the gifts. Jedidiah paused for a moment to observe the young men as they ate. It was the old man's custom to ask questions of his guest during breakfast. Matt and Jackson were no exception. "I am glad that you are here. I don't want you to take offense by my questions, for it is part of my duty as the caretaker of this realm. Helping people understand the condition of their hearts and the motives of their minds is what I do. Of course, you do not have to answer. The questions are for heart probing," said Jedidiah.

"By all means, Sir, please ask away," said Matt. He was smiling from ear to ear, eager to hear what the old man was going to ask.

However, Jackson was uneasy about the whole thing. He didn't like the idea of anyone probing his mind or getting into his business.

Jedidiah did not respond to either of the young men's reactions but simply started his routine. "What I am about to ask you will be a delight to you or a threat, depending on what you value. There are seven things a man must be aware of in life, for they either will please his Maker or displease Him. Now, the first question. Do you view yourself better than others?"

Matt thought hard about the question while Jackson burst into laughter. He thought to himself, *How could a man with so much wealth ask a question about being better than others. Surely, this old man must think himself higher than anyone else with all he has.*

"Is there something humorous about the question?" asked Jedidiah.

"No, just thinking about the question," replied Jackson. The old man understood what Jackson was implying and made no comment. He simply continued his inquiry.

"I shall ask the questions, and if you would allow me to finish, you may answer or ask me whatever you desire." The old man opened his book and began reading. "Do you think that a person should lie or kill the innocent?" Not allowing a comment from the men, he continued with his questions. "Do you think it is right to devise wicked schemes against others? Do you think it is right to agree with evil people or join them in their efforts to condemn the innocent, knowing that they have done no wrong? And my last question is… Are you the kind of man who would cause discord among people?"

After Jedidiah had finished, both men looked as though they were in deep thought. It was certainly a lot to ponder, and his words made each man search his own soul, however tarnished or clear it was. Jedidiah paused to let them think about his questions as he poured more milk and juice into the glasses and piled on hotcakes with homemade maple, buttered syrup. The aroma itself made them eager to indulge themselves. It was Jedidiah's delight to see young men enjoy the food he had prepared. The young men showed their appreciation by scarfing down the hotcakes like it was their last meal.

After breakfast, Matt felt better and stronger than he had ever felt before in his life. The breakfast had also given new vitality to Jackson. He now was wide awake and felt like everything was going to be fine even though the questions made him uneasy. Matt asked Jedidiah what kind of breakfast he had fixed for them because he felt supercharged. Jedidiah laughed and looked very pleased that the young men had enjoyed the breakfast and said that it was the prayer that added the extra spice.

Now that breakfast was over, the three of them walked to the front door and stepped through. Outside, things were the same. When they turned around to look at the house, it had reverted back to a large tree. The young men were amazed at how a tree could turn into a house and not just any house but a mansion. It was so unreal, yet they had spent the night there. The old man laughed because he knew they were flabbergasted at what they had seen. Jackson's biggest concern was about his hidden treasure and how he was going to retrieve it now that he was outside, and the treasure was inside.

Jedidiah took them to the fields that he had told them about and gave them instructions on how he wanted things done. He told them that everything had to be done exactly as he instructed, or they would not receive the gift they desired. Jedidiah watched to see if his words took root or fell on unresponsive ears. He said, "Look at the fields. They have been cultivated and prepared for the planting. They are empty right now. However, if you follow my instruction and work hard all day, there will be plenty of food for all the villages in my land. Your job will be to sow and plant the seeds located in those crates to your right. This has to be done by the end of the day. There cannot be one seed left in the crates. Your fields are divided into sections. You must plant the right seeds in each section. If you do not, the food will be ruined. Plant only in the fields that are assigned to you. You each have a field and a half to plant, and it must be done before the sun sets." Jedidiah looked at them so intensely that both men could feel the ground under their feet tremble. "Do you understand your assignment?" he asked them.

The young men acknowledged that they understood.

"Now, one more thing," said Jedidiah cautiously. "Every hour, you must take 15 minutes to refresh yourselves. The work, at times, can get very hard, and you may become physically fatigued. I have prepared for you special water and food. If you will obey my words, you will accomplish your task," explained Jedidiah.

"The fields are so large. I don't know if we will get all of this done in one day," complained Jackson.

"You are right, Jackson. The fields are large, but they have been chosen especially for each of you. If you will look around, you will see that there are many other fields that I could have chosen for you. The ones you have are the best for you."

Matt looked out over the fields and concluded that the fields were large, but if the old man said it could be done, he was going to give it his best effort. "Come on, Jackson. Jedidiah believes it can be done, so let's get to it."

"One more thing, young Men. You must do your own work. No exceptions. Any man who doesn't work to provide for his family and himself isn't worth tasteless salt."

"Yes, Sir," they replied.

"Let me say it again. You must do your own work. Even if one of you gets tired, the other is forbidden from helping. Do you understand?" he asked again.

The young men nodded that they did.

"Very well. I will leave you to your work and will return at sundown."

Jedidiah made his way back toward the large tree, humming a catchy tune that seemed to energize everything around him. The birds joined in along with bees, buzzing wildly like they also had work to do.

The men were inspired to get started. Off they went toward their respective fields. As they reach the crates, they were amazed by how many bags of seed were in them. There were 10 bags in each crate, and each bag had 100 pounds of seed. There were 30 crates total, 10 for each field. Each crate had the name of the seed posted on the outside, indicating where the seed was to be planted.

The sun had risen just above the mountain top. Birds and other critters could be heard doing whatever they did to take care of their own families. Matt and Jackson looked around for tools to open the crates but found none.

"How are we supposed to get to the seed? Open these crates with our bare hands?" complained Jackson.

"I don't know. Let's give it a try," said Matt. With one pull, Matt tore open the first crate and started laughing. "Wow! Whatever was in that breakfast must have given us the strength to get the job done, so let's do it."

Jackson, too, found that it was easy to rip open the crates as well as the bags of seed. Matt blocked off their assigned work areas and began to plant and sow the first rows. The first seed had vegetables of like nature that could be planted together without harm, like peas and corn. As the corn grew, it would provide a stalk to allow the vine from the peas a place to cling to as they grew. The amazing thing they discovered was that, whenever the seed hit the ground, the ground automatically closed over the seed.

Jackson was doing well also. Each hour, they took a break and refreshed themselves as Jedidiah had instructed them. However, by noon, Jackson became more fatigued and began to fall behind in his work. Matt had completed three fourths of his first field and was on his way back to take a break as he saw that Jackson was falling further and further behind.

"Hey, Jackson, let's take a break. You missed the last one, so come on and take a break to refresh yourself."

"I can't take a break right now. I'm too far behind. I'll catch the next one."

"No! Jackson, Jedidiah said we have to take the breaks every hour. I can see how the heat and fatigue is weighing you down. You need to take a break."

Jackson would not listen to Matt. He knew that, if he didn't get the seed in the ground by sundown, he would forfeit whatever gift that was coming to him. He said to himself, *I should have gotten more rest last night. I'm so tired and even the food and refreshment that Jedidiah provided for us is not enough to keep the tiredness out of my body.*

After Matt had his 15-minute break, he went back to work. Two hours before sundown, he had completed his entire task. It was a hard day's work, but he felt good about it. Matt looked over to see how Jackson was progressing and could see that he had only finished one field. Matt knew that, at the pace Jackson was going, he would never finish his task. He wanted to help him; however, he remembered the strict instruction Jedidiah had given to them… that each man must complete his own work. How could Matt let Jackson suffer the loss of not getting the gift for which he had worked so hard? Didn't they both come together, and weren't they comrades laboring together for the same thing? Shouldn't he help a friend in need? All these thoughts filled Matt's mind. Nevertheless, he knew in his heart that it was still better to obey Jedidiah's instruction than to let his own heart get in the way.

Jackson struggled. He had only taken three of the ten breaks he was supposed to refresh himself with, and now, the fatigue was more than he could bear. He looked over and saw Matt standing on the edge of the field, waving his hands. He then heard him say, "Come on in, and take a break to refresh yourself. You can't do the rest unless you get some energy." Jackson would not listen. He thought he could at least finish half of the last field and then take a break. One hour before sunset, he finally took a break and gained enough energy to try and to finish the last of the planting. He looked at the last crate and thought, *Jedidiah said the seed must go in the right row, but as long as it's in the same field, I don't see what difference it would make as long as they are planted. If I just throw them over the field, they will grow. Then, I will be finished on time.*

Matt saw what Jackson was about to do and shouted to him that it would be a mistake. "You can't mix the seed. You have to plant them in the order of the crates." He clearly heard what Matt said. However, Jackson would not listen. He carelessly took the rest of the seed and sowed it wherever it went.

By the end of the day, as the sun was setting, he completed the task just in time. Right on time, over the hill came Jedidiah in a wagon to retrieve the two tired workers. With him, he had cool water and freshly baked cakes that would hold them over until the evening meal.

"Greetings, my Friends. I see that you have completed your tasks. By the looks of you, I'd say a well-earned rest is in order.

Come and sit. Rest and take all the drink and food you desire. I only have with me bread cakes and a little water to wash them down. The men took turns washing their faces and hands. The water was exhilarating. Not only did the fresh water clean the dirt off their hands, but it had a deep and unrecognizable taste that quickly quenched their thirst.

Jedidiah watched them as they sat down with him to eat the cakes. "Well, young Men, let me tell you what you have just done." They both looked at Jedidiah as if he knew what Jackson had done and was about to chastise him. Instead, he told them how thrilled he was that they had completed the work. He told them how all the villagers in the valleys depended on the food collected from the fields, particularly from the 10 valleys in the southern part. They depended on it the most because the famine there was most severe. Matt looked at Jackson, waiting for him to confess to Jedidiah about the last field. However, no such confession was made.

Later that evening, when they returned to the tree, Jackson went to Jedidiah, requesting an audience with him. Jedidiah invited him into a large sitting room with a beautiful fireplace and nice, comfortable chairs. Jackson took a seat next to the old man and began to share with him about what had happened in the field. He told Jedidiah about how he and Matt were doing well together the first part of the day and how they both took great care in planting the seed. But in the afternoon, he said, Matt started to fall behind in his work and had problems catching up. He explained how he tried to encourage Matt to take breaks but that Matt was so driven to get the job done that he neglected to refresh himself every hour like they had been instructed. Consequently, Matt fell behind and deviated from the given instructions.

Jedidiah did not say anything but just listened as Jackson continued to tell the events of the day. Jackson went on with his story while Matt was busy sorting out piles of letters that came in to Jedidiah from the villages. The letters had come in over the past year, expressing gratitude for all that Jedidiah had done for them over the years. Jedidiah sat in his chair while Jackson continued.

"Matt was frantic, knowing he only had one more hour to finish his part of the field. What he did next shocked me," stated Jackson. "He started to plant the remaining seed everywhere. He mixed them and threw them all over the field until they were all gone. I shouted at him and told him that he had to stop and do it the right way. He just wouldn't listen. Finally, I gave up and hoped for the best. I know that you told us to do it the right way, but I know how hard it was for me, so I understand why Matt did what he did. I tried to stop him, but he said that he wanted the gift and that was all that mattered. I would have helped him, but you told us not to help each other, so I obeyed."

After Jackson said all he had to say, he dismissed himself from Jedidiah's presence. Jedidiah thanked Jackson and asked him to keep quiet about the day's activities and that he would address Matt later regarding the task.

That evening before dinner, Jackson entered his room to check on his hidden treasure. He felt good about what he had collected. The only thing left was the treasure box under the Sun Stone. He planned to wait until after supper before collecting it. His hope was that no one would suspect anything before he was well on his way. The plan was to escape without notice. In the meantime, he headed toward the dining area.

The old man sat across from Matt and Jackson at dinner, looking intently at both of them. Jedidiah was deeply disturbed by Jackson's report and decided to address it. "Matt, I am told that you had some trouble today in the field. Is that so?" asked the old man.

"I guess both of us are a little tired after all that work, Sir, but we got it done," replied Matt.

"That you did, and I must say that the fields assigned to you look good. Did you follow my instructions to the letter?"

Matt was a little puzzled and paused to wait for Jackson to answer, but he never did. Jackson knew that Matt wouldn't say anything to expose him, but it was possible that he would say something in his own defense. In order to prevent him from doing so, Jackson, unwilling to risk exposure, quickly twisted things around. He told the old man how Matt and he had worked well together before, but for some reason, not as well today.

"Matt got a little confused and put the wrong seed in the last half of the field," Jackson said.

Matt was shocked and started to protest, but the pleading look on Jackson's face stopped him. Matt knew that Jackson's family needed the treasure gift more than he and his parents. It was true that everyone in the village was going through a famine, but some were struggling more than others. Jackson's family was one of the poorest. Without food and provision, they would soon die. Matt kept the truth to himself but did not lie to cover for Jackson.

"Is it true, Matt? Did you mix the seed in the field?" asked Jedidiah.

Matt did not say anything. He only looked at Jackson with disappointment and sadly turned his head from the old man.

"Then, it's true. You mixed the seed and did not tell me. Oh, my dear young Friend. This is not good. You must show me where you sowed it so we may sort it out before it's too late."

Matt was angry at Jackson for putting him in such a compromising position. He felt betrayed by Jackson and felt that he had let Jedidiah down.

"Sir, let Jackson show you where the seeds are mixed because he is aware of where they are located."

"You are not aware of where they are located? I thought you were the one who mixed them up."

"No, Sir. I followed your instructions to the letter," said Matt.

"Then, why did Jackson accuse you of doing so?"

"I'm afraid you will have to ask Jackson that question, Sir," Matt replied.

The old man was not pleased at what he heard and set out to correct the error immediately. When he turned to address Jackson, he could not be found. Jackson knew his time was limited, so he set out to make the most of it. Going back to his room, he decided he should add the Sun Stone and the silver treasure box to his collection as soon as possible. As he sat on his bed trying to think of an explanation that he could give Jedidiah, his door opened. There in front of him stood Jedidiah and Matt. Jedidiah didn't address Jackson regarding what he had done but urged him to join Matt and he to go to the field in order to correct the disastrous deed he had done. Reluctantly, Jackson went with them.

They worked most of the night redistributing the seed. It was Jedidiah who did most of the work. He knew the intricate details about how seed and soil worked, and with his knowledge, he re-arranged everything. It was like magic. The seed and soil rose as the wind swirled, separating them until all was in its right order. Matt and Jackson stood amazed, and there was no question that the old man was more than he made himself out to be. Jedidiah sat down to take a rest. The work had taken strength out of him, and he needed a moment to recover. Matt brought water and sat down next to him to make sure that all was well. It was the perfect opportunity for Jackson to take his loot and leave.

Jackson headed back to the tree and stood in front as the old man did, remembering what Jedidiah had said and done. He raised his hand and repeated the words he had heard, but the door did not appear. Jackson did it again, and still it did not work. Then, he remembered what the old man had said when he gave him the cup of tea. "As a man thinks in his heart so he is… If you believe and do not doubt, it will happen." Jackson did believe, and just like the tea turned into strong wine, so the door appeared and opened before him. He knew exactly what he needed to do. Without hesitation, he grabbed his sack and headed for the room that contained the Sun Stone and the silver box. When he arrived, he found them to be right where he saw them last. He cautiously approached, hoping the weird growls and sounds would not return.

Jedidiah realized what Jackson was up to and alerted Matt. He urged Matt to run quickly after Jackson to prevent him from entering the Sun Stone room. As Matt ran, he heard Jedidiah yelling, "You must not let him enter, for if he does, he will never come out again!" Matt ran like the wind to reach the house which had not yet changed back to a tree.

Once inside, he ran down the hall to the room that housed the Sun Stone. He stopped and called for Jackson to come out if he was in there. When Jedidiah reached Matt, he looked in as Matt stood by his side. They both stood at the edge of the door. Matt dared not take another step. What he saw terrified him. There before him was his friend, Jackson, holding a bag in one hand with the silver treasure box under his arm. Evidently, the Sun Stone had been put into the bag.

With his other hand, Jackson was trying to dodge the claws and fangs of the largest cat-like beast Matt had ever seen. It was ferocious with eyes that looked straight through the object it stared at. The large rug in the middle of the room was tingling with imperceptible sounds. Matt had seen several of these kind of rugs throughout the mansion. The beast had taken hold of Jackson and was pulling him into the rug. Jackson screamed and struggled to keep from entering the rug, yet he still held onto the loot in his hand. He saw the old man's face clearly for the first time. What he saw frightened him even more. He knew that his pleading would not prevail because he was staring Justice in the face. However, he pleaded with him just the same. Jedidiah stayed in his place even when Jackson cried to him for mercy.

Jackson knew that his time was short and called to Matt to help him. Of course, Matt's kind heart would not allow him to stand by and see Jackson devoured by what he could only describe as a cat rug. When Matt took a step toward Jackson, the old man put out his hand to stop him.

"You cannot help him, Matt. He has chosen his way, and there is nothing you or I can do about it."

As Jackson screamed and struggled to get away, he dropped the bag and box and fought to get away from the beast that now consumed him. The last scream from Jackson sounded like it came from a bottomless pit. When Matt looked again, things appeared normal except that, in the rug, another form was added. It was Jackson in the mouth of the great cat woven into the rug.

"What happened to him? Where did he go?" asked Matt.

"As you can see, my young Friend, he chose to join the others in the rugs of greed."

"What others? I didn't see others?" said Matt.

"Look closely, my Friend, you will see them," replied Jedidiah.

Matt looked very closely at the rug and discovered that there were other people woven into the rug. "Why are they there?" he asked. "Why would you do such a thing?"

"I told you when you came to me that you did not have to pay anything to get the gift. I also explained that what you had would do."

"You both agreed to follow my instructions to the letter. You did, but Jackson did not. Even when I gave him a chance to tell the truth, he continued to slander, lie, and blame you for his failures," said Jedidiah.

Matt had a surprised look on his face as Jedidiah told him about everything Jackson had done. The old man was very wise and was able to see into each man's heart. He knew from the start what each man would do.

Matt was not pleased with what Jackson had done, but he didn't want him to be lost in a rug for the rest of his life. Something had to be done. How was he going to explain to Jackson's mother that her son was not coming back? He asked Jedidiah what was going to happen to him. The old man explained to Matt that it was not right for Jackson to lie about what he had done and then blame it on others. He said that Jackson chose the way of treachery and deceit. He told him that he and Jackson traveled different paths. "You took the way of honor and truth, and Jackson took the way of those who are forever imprisoned in the rug of greed," the old man explained. "Do you see the paintings that line this hallway?"

"Yes, I remember them," said Matt.

"They also chose the hard way and were consumed by the walls in payment for their betrayal. No one who deliberately plots evil will leave this house. They were offered a gift just like you and Jackson. They choose to rob, steal, and would have killed to get what they wanted. This is not the way of truth. Therefore, it cannot be tolerated. Those who have been captured by their greed and hateful hearts will receive their reward. You and many others like you have chosen the good part, and it shall not be taken from you."

Matt understood all that Jedidiah had spoken to him, yet his heart was heavy for the loss of Jackson. He was wondering whether or not he should speak more on the matter or be silent. To be silent would not help Jackson or the others who had entered the old man's home with evil intent. However, to speak on their behalf may show contempt for the old man and the way of truth. Nevertheless, Matt found himself addressing Jedidiah without actually knowing what to say.

"Master, Jedidiah," he said, bowing himself to the ground. "Yes, my Son? What is it that you want?"

Son? Why did he call me Son? Matt wondered, but he was not going to let the opportunity slip by. He quickly changed the way he was addressing Jedidiah. "May I speak, my Father?" Matt asked, still not knowing what to say.

"Yes, by all means… Speak, my Son."

The old man's approval gave Matt courage to speak. He just hoped that what he had to say would make sense. Jedidiah took a nearby chair and sat down right in front of Matt. Then, he waited for Matt to begin. Matt held his breath and then let it out slowly. "Well, my Lord…" he began. "I do not know what crimes the others have committed against you. I perceive in order to be in such a predicament, their crimes must have been tremendously serious. You have been patient and shown only kindness."

Jedidiah held up his hand to stop Matt from speaking. He informed Matt that he was not the one that Jackson sinned against but God.

"I know that what Jackson did was completely out of order and has greatly offended the Lord. However, I know that the Lord is merciful, and if you will help me speak to the Lord on Jackson's behalf, maybe something can be done."

Jedidiah showed no anger at Matt's request. However, he did wonder why Matt seem to be so obsessed with helping a man who deliberately tried to frame and destroy him. Things became clearer as Matt told the old man the story behind why he had to save Jackson's life.

At one time, the mothers of Matt and Jackson were best friends. A dispute over food and provisions for the village caused friction between their husbands, and a heated conflict ensued. As emotions rose, words were thrown like daggers between the two husbands. Suddenly, a voice from the crowd yelled, "Look, all the food is gone… What about my children?" With that statement, violence soon followed. Several members of the village died from all the pushing and shoving over food rationing.

Matt's father had been given the task of rationing the food, and Jackson's father was a volunteer helper. Both men were trampled underfoot by the embellished statement that all the food was gone. Of course, it was not true, but when people panic, reasoning dissipates. The people were very sorry after things calmed down, but the damage had already been done, and several people died. Both Matt's and Jackson's fathers had been seriously injured. Jackson's mother, Junia, blamed Matt's father because he was over the rationing, and she felt that he should have been better prepared for the crowd. Her anger and bitterness got the better of her, and soon, formed a wedge between her and Frances, Matt's mother. The whole incident was unusual. It was the first time anything like it had ever happened.

Jeremy, Matt's father, tried his best to reconcile the two families, but Junia could not find it in her heart to forgive. Nevertheless, Jeremy offered Jack, Jackson's father, a job cutting trees, hoping that one day their relationship would mend. Unfortunately, Jack came to work one day intoxicated and had climbed high in a tree across from where Jeremy was working on a half-cut limb. When Jeremy realized that Jack was half drunk, he ordered him to go down. Jack refused, accusing Jeremy of hindering him from a day's wage. Jeremy explained that he would pay him for the day if he climbed down. Jack refused and took hold of the limb Jeremy was working on but lost his footing. The limb broke off, taking Jack down with it. By the time Jeremy reached him, Jack was already dead.

When Junia received the news of her husband's death, she went into a rage. She accused the Loman family of murdering her husband even after a dozen witnesses testified that Jack was at fault. The authorities ruled it a careless accident. "As God is my witness, I'll see that you pay" were her last words to Frances and Jeremy before she isolated herself away from everyone.

Matt and Jackson remained friends despite their mothers' broken friendship. How could he go home and tell Jackson's mother that her son wasn't coming back? Matt knew it would destroy her to have lost a husband and now her son. After Matt told his story to Jedidiah, he raised his head and asked what he could do to get Jackson out of the rug.

Jedidiah spoke softly to Matt, telling him how sorry he felt over his loss. But it did not change the fact that Jackson and the others trapped in the rug had violated the law of truth. Matt grew frustrated, and Jedidiah was well aware of it. However, he waited for a response from Matt.

"What if I give up my gift?" Matt asked.

Jedidiah had never had anyone make a request to give up a gift. He could see the struggle in Matt's face. Giving up the gift meant giving up his share of the food and treasure which they both knew he needed. How would his family manage through the winter months? How would they survive? It meant living on the last little substance he and his parents had put away in case he and Jackson failed to get work.

Jedidiah looked intently at Matt and asked him if he really wanted to trade the life support he had so diligently worked to obtain for his family in exchange for a man who betrayed and framed him.

Matt simply said, "If I go back without him, what will I tell his mother?"

Matt's words touched the old man. It showed him what he already knew about Matt. He was a man of compassion. The tears in Jedidiah's eyes showed Matt that he understood. "I'll tell you what, Matt... If you give up all that you have worked for—the food in the fields, the treasure gift in your possession, and spend one year here in my home as my servant—I will pray for Jackson's release. Also, you may not go back to visit your parents until the task has been completed. I will give you one hour to think it over."

The old man turned and walked away, leaving Matt standing in the middle of the room, pondering over the decision he had to make. If he stayed and did as Jedidiah wanted, his parents would not know what happened to him. Jackson would certainly be the hero of the day, bringing back all the food and provision for everyone except his parents who would have to wait in poverty until his return. *Jackson had not proven to be a loyal friend. Why would he be concerned about what happens to the people at home? He's the kind of person who would fabricate some wild story that I got eaten by some beast.* Matt thought about all the things that could go wrong back home. One thing was for certain. If he did not stay, Jackson would not get out of the rug, and his mother would not have her son.

When Jedidiah returned, he was already aware of Matt's decision. "So you have chosen to stay?" he asked. It was more of a statement than a question. "Yes, Father, I have decided to stay."

"Very well. I will see to it that Jackson is released, but he will not remember this place. However, he will have periodic glimpses of being devoured by the rug of greed. Hopefully, it will teach him a valuable lesson regarding honor."

Matt was relieved to hear the good news. "What about the food and provisions for the villages? Will the famine continue? Will my people get through this season?"

The old man smiled at Matt, whose thoughts were never about himself but always about others. Jedidiah assured Matt that, not only would the villages have plenty of food and provisions, but they were going to have an overflow. There was an emotional release in Matt's face. One could say a glowing smile appeared, even if it was for only a brief second.

Chapter 4

PREPARATION

Afterreemerging from the rug, Jackson found himself in the middle of a field near home and had no idea how he had gotten there. He didn't even know the time of day it was or what he was supposed to have been doing. When he walked into his home, his mother embraced him like she had not seen him for years. She hadn't. Jackson, according to his mother, had been gone for two years. In the time he was gone, the village had prospered in food and in growth.

Things had changed some, but not so much that Jackson couldn't recognize everything. There was one thing more that had changed, and his mother noticed it right away. "Jackson, what happened to you? Where have you been?" she asked him.

He was not able to tell her because he could not remember. His memory was foggy, and past details were hard to grasp. He was aware that he had been through an extreme ordeal. However, the ordeal remained a mystery. He felt strange. The state of his heart now contrasted with his previous self-centeredness and pride. He could not remember what had happened to Matt, his friend, but he knew that Matt had done something great in his life and had made a tremendous sacrifice for him. In return, Jackson felt he had to take care of Matt's parents for as long as Matt was away.

*****

Matt rose early every morning and gave thanks to God before setting out to accomplish the work Jedidiah set before him. In six months, Matt had planted 180 fields. Each field was larger than the ones he and Jackson had planted previously.

Matt was pleased with the work he had accomplished, and so was Jedidiah, who often told him so. Matt's strength doubled, his endurance tripled, and he grew to be three inches taller than Jedidiah, placing him at 6'4" tall. He teased the old man by standing in front of him, going up and down on his toes. The old man laughed and thumped him on the head with his staff. Wincing, Matt would rub the bruise for instant relief. The old man would say, "It's just a reminder for you not to think of yourself more highly than you ought to." Matt would laugh and pat Jedidiah teasingly on the head.

Matt's height was not the only noticeable change. Working in the fields for months and consuming food from Jedidiah's table caused his physical appearance to change. It was like he had been chiseled out of a rock. There was power in his arms that could easily lift the wagon he and the old man traveled on, and his legs were strong enough to carry it for miles. He was noticeably handsome with tanned skin from working in the sun. Even though he often was teased by Jedidiah, his kind heart kept him unassuming. It was evident that Matt had grown both in stature and wisdom. They laughed often, and Matt affectionately would wrap his arms around the old man who had become his dear friend.

The land had changed Matt completely. He had become very fond of Jedidiah who taught him more about life in six months than he had learned in his now 21 years. The old man grew to love Matt like a son. Of course, Matt felt the same way about Jedidiah. Even from the start, the old seer had seen in Matt a good heart. What Matt didn't know was that Jedidiah was training him for far better things in life than he ever could have dreamed. The time was almost right, and in the next six months, Matt would be ready for the challenges ahead of him.

Chapter 5

THE GRANDDAUGHTER

At the beginning of Matt's last six months, a young woman of extraordinary beauty came to visit Jedidiah. She had long, dark hair and flawless, brown skin. Her whole form revealed beauty, strength, and grace. Even from a distance, Matt could tell she was regal and one of a kind. He stood in the middle of the field just staring in her direction until Jedidiah touched him on the shoulder. Matt jumped, almost tripping over the garden tool in his hand, unaware that Jedidiah had come up behind him.

"You should whistle, talk, or sing... coming up behind someone like that. You made me jump out of my boots!" Matt said, laughing at himself.

Jedidiah laughed, too. He could see that Matt was gazing at the young woman near the tree. When she raised her hand, the tree took the form of a house, and she waited as the door appeared. As was her custom, she reached over to put her hand on the old house cat and rubbed under his chin and behind his ear. The old cat purred like a kitten, happy to see her.

Matt was surprised that she knew how to gain access to the house. "Who is she?" he asked Jedidiah.

"She is my granddaughter. She comes here each year about this season to spend time with me. Her mother usually comes with her. I see that, this time, she is alone."

"But she looks…" Matt paused, trying to think of what to say.

"Looks darker than me?" said Jedidiah.

"Well, yes. But…"

"You have a problem with that?" asked Jedidiah, toying with him.

"No, Sir, that's not what I was going to say." Matt was afraid that he had offended the old seer and was trying to straighten things out.

"Then, what were you going to say?" asked Jedidiah, chuckling under his breath.

"I was going to say that, in all my life, I've never seen anyone more beautiful," he explained, turning to feast his eyes once more on her as she went inside.

"Well, I guess I can let you off the hook after that remark," he said jokingly. "Come with me, and I will introduce you to my granddaughter."

Matt was thunderstruck. He thought, *What in the world am I going to say to a lady like Jedidiah's granddaughter?* He had spent hours in Jedidiah's library, learning things he never thought would come into his grasp. He was so grateful and humbled by the opportunity. His experience living with Jedidiah so far had been a great adventure. Meeting his granddaughter would be the culmination of a dream come true.

The old man could see the sweat coming from Matt's brow, which made him smile. He placed his hand on Matt's shoulder and assured him that his granddaughter would not bite. Matt tried to laugh it off, but a little anxiety got caught in his throat. Clearing his throat, he said, "I'm not sure I'm ready for this. Look at me. I'm dirty and smelly from the fields and…"

"Matt, you just finished work, and you are dirty because you work hard," said the old man, sighing.

"I know… But no woman wants to talk to a dirty man, especially the first time she meets him."

Jedidiah tried to calm him, but his efforts were not working. Matt insisted that he be allowed to at least take a bath and groom himself before meeting her. Jedidiah agreed, laughing at Matt's jittery reaction. He told Matt he was surprised that he let a young woman intimidate him so much. Matt didn't find it humorous. Arching his brow, he asked, "By the way, what's her name?"

"Her name is Patience," Jedidiah said, laughing. "Something you need a lot of," he mused as they moved toward the house.

Walking toward the house, Matt's mind was suddenly invaded by thoughts of his parents, especially of his mother. He often thought about them. Only this time, it was different. This time, the thoughts lingered.

*****

In a small cottage on the outskirts of the village, Columbidae, a woman sat, rocking in an old wooden chair on a humbly made porch. Her graceful voice pierced the air as she sung one of the songs from an old hymn book. It was one that brought back fond memories. In her solitude, she raised her eyes to the sky and whispered a small prayer. "God, please take care of my boy. Please bring him home." A small tear trickled down her face. The thought of not seeing him was more than she could bear.

Suddenly, a tall man quietly walked up and called her name. "Frances…?"

Startled, she rose, not knowing what to think at first. Then, she gave a brief smile and walked toward her husband of 30 years.

With arms open, the large man grabbed his wife intently and with love in his eyes said, "You are thinking of Matt… Aren't you?"

Smiling and barely controlling her tears, she replied, "Oh, Jeremy… You know me so well. I'm just praying that Matt will come home soon."

With compassion, he held her close, whispering in her ear, "Have faith, my Darling. He will return soon. I can just feel it."

Frances and Jeremy had no idea where Matt was or how to find him.

Jackson had become like a second son to them. Jeremy still was not able to work full-time because of his previous injury during the food rationing incident. After the death of Jackson's father, it was a miracle that Jackson even wanted to be near them. Jeremy wanted to help Junia and Jackson as much as he could, but Junia would have nothing to do with them. Revenge was the only thought on her mind, and sooner or later, she was going to have it. She had no more regard or friendship left in her for Frances and Jeremy. Yet Jackson had proven to be very helpful, desperately trying to mend the relationship between his mother and Matt's parents.

*****

When Matt walked out of his room, heading for the dining area, he could hear his stomach growling and could smell the delicious aroma. He heard the familiar voice of Jedidiah, laughing and talking with his granddaughter. The thought of stepping around the corner into the dining room made him feel uncomfortable. However, hearing laughter from Patience eased his tension. Standing in the doorway, thinking about whether he should spoil the mood, abruptly he was snatched back to reality when he heard a cheerful voice loud and clear.

"Well, hello there, Matt. About time you got yourself in here," said Jedidiah teasingly.

Matt was not amused. It seemed like everything Jedidiah said embarrassed him.

"Matt, this is Patience, my beautiful granddaughter."

Nervously gazing into the woman's eyes, Matt was unable to speak. He hadn't seen a woman as beautiful as Patience in his entire life. He didn't know if he should reach out to shake her hand or bow.

"What's wrong with you, Son? Say something." The old man cackled.

Matt's mind seemed to stop working. He wasn't sure what to say, and Jedidiah was having the time of his life watching Matt squirm. Studying Matt's awkward appearance, Patience broke the silence by extending her hand to Matt in greeting. Nervously, Matt forced himself to shake the woman's hand. With a nervous gasp, he thought, *her hand is so slender and soft.* As their hands touched, he lifted his eyes, surprise written on his face. Their eyes locked, and he felt a warmth go through his body. There is something about this woman that drew him to her. *Why am I so nervous?* he asked himself. *I've seen plenty of girls in Columbidae, not as beautiful, but still...* Matt's wondering mind was interrupted by a familiar voice.

"It's about time one of you did something. The food is getting cold. Sit down, Matt, and stop blushing," Jedidiah said, watching both of them in amusement. "Oh, by the way, Matt… Did you know that my granddaughter was a princess?"

Matt didn't know what to say. And Jedidiah didn't give him much of a chance to speak as he continued talking.

"Steven, her father, is king of the Ethiopians. His anointing from God enabled him to kill two man-eating lions that ravaged many villages. His courage and selfless dedication to helping his people gained him great respect from all the tribes in the East. That's how his parents, as missionaries, were able to win thousands of their people to Christ. So be aware that you have been blessed to sit in the presence of a princess." Jedidiah chuckled as he took a drink of ice-cold tea.

Patience had had enough of her grandfather's teasing Matt and told him so. Jedidiah smiled at her and asked what she thought of Matt. "He is a fine-looking young man… Don't you think, Honey?"

Patience blushed and gave her grandfather a kiss on the head. She knew exactly what he was doing. "Poppy, I think it's time for us to say grace and have our dinner. Don't you?"

He laughed as Matt stood to pull the chair out for Patience.

"Thank you, Matt. I appreciate your courtesy," she said, smiling.

Matt felt like Jacob in the Bible when he first saw Rachel. It was the closest thing to love at first sight. "You are very welcome," he replied.

After the prayer, Patience asked Matt where he was from and about his family and how he had come to know her grandfather. Once Matt started talking, his tension went away. As the conversation went on, both he and Patience found themselves enjoying each other's company. Jedidiah was pleased that his granddaughter was having a delightful time and with a young man that he adored.

"Poppy tells me that you have another six months to spend with him," she said, probing to see his reaction. "That's right. Master Jedidiah has been more than kind, letting me stay on to work things out." Matt did not go into details about the arrangement he and Jedidiah had made. He didn't tell her why he came and about the debt he was required to repay.

"Patience, why don't you tell Matt why you came to see me."

She looked at the old man like he had lost his mind. "Poppy, I'm sure that Matt would rather hear about something more interesting than me."

When she turned to observe Matt's demeanor, he was looking straight at her. What Patience didn't know or had not taken the time to observe was that Matt had been looking at her since the first time he laid eyes on her. Another blush told Matt that she seemed to be interested in him as well.

"Is it a secret?" he asked.

"Is what a secret?" she replied.

"Why you came here to see your grandfather."

Patience didn't know what to say. She had come because her grandfather had sent for her. Although she and her mother usually came together, he had insisted that she come as soon as she could. In all her years, she never had disobeyed him. It was not because he spoiled her but because of her love and adoration. She loved him deeply and so came immediately at his call. Ever since she was born, Jedidiah had been telling her that she was his favorite grandchild. Of course, he said that to all of his grandchildren when the others were not around. It was a game they played. However, Patience was very special because she was the first born and the only girl. She had the same spirit of serving as her grandfather. She had undying devotion toward her Lord and toward her grandfather.

"To answer your question, Poppy... You know very well why I came, mainly to keep you out of trouble until mother arrives."

"So it wasn't just to come and see an old man?" replied Jedidiah.

"There is nothing old about you, Poppy, you old jokester," she laughed. "I know that look of mischief. Even when I was a little girl, I could tell. So, what are you planning?"

Matt was amused by how Patience and Jedidiah teased each other. There was more than a blood connection between them. It was more like on a spiritual level. He couldn't put his finger on it, but he could feel it. He had a feeling that this kind of play was routine with them. He cleared his throat and got their attention. Patience and Jedidiah looked at each other and realized they were leaving him out of their conversation even if he didn't say anything.

After dinner, Jedidiah led them to the sitting room, a room surrounded by windows where one could look out and see for miles in one direction and only a few feet in another. The wonders of nature surrounded them—land, sea, and sky. At night, the moon and millions of stars could be seen. During the day, trees and flowers of every kind could be seen, and if the windows were opened, the sweet fragrance from them spilled into the room.

It was time for Jedidiah to explain why he had sent for Patience and why it was important for Matt to meet her. For years, Jedidiah had been planning a special surprise for his granddaughter, and the time was almost right for him to give it to her. Patience sat comfortably on a hand-carved love seat designed by the old man himself. Woodwork was one of his many specialties, something Matt was not aware of. Because there was no other place to sit, Matt asked for permission to sit next to Patience. Before Patience could consent, Jedidiah motioned with his hand for Matt to sit next to her. Patience blushed, moving a little to the right to give Matt ample room to sit comfortably.

Matt was not the only one who had been stealing glances all evening. Patience was very much taken by Matt's strong demeanor. Not only was he tall and handsome like her father, she found him to be more intelligent than he let on. Yes, he was quiet, but behind that quietness was a spirit that loved God and cared for people. As they talked, she found that she was attracted mostly to his heart. There was this atmosphere around him that just allowed her to be herself. He felt the same about her and wondered if a friendship between them was possible.

"Now, my little Jewel..." Jedidiah said, looking straight at Patience. "All these years, your Poppy has been planning this special gift for you. Many years have passed, and many things have happened. And today, the good Lord in His wisdom has given me the sign." He paused, giving his words time to resonate in her mind.

"What kind of a sign are we talking about, Poppy? Road, sky, or space?" she asked.

Jedidiah laughed at her and continued as if she had not said anything. "I will let you know at the end of six months what the gift is, and you will have to stay with me for the duration of that time."

Patience leaned forward in the seat as if to rise, but the seat held her fast. "What is this, Poppy? What's going on with this love seat?" exclaimed Patience.

Matt was concerned and tried to stand to help her out of the seat but found that he, too, was held fast. Jedidiah laughed and assured them that they were fine. Jedidiah had made the love seat out of special flowers, spices, and a secret ingredient from the Holy Book that identified certain compatible traits in people.

Jedidiah had in mind that Matt and Patience were meant for each other from the first time he met Matt. Unlike Jackson, Matt was selfless and considerate of others before himself. He was the kind of man Jedidiah wanted for his granddaughter. He had prayed for 19 years since the day she was born that God would send the right man just as he had done for her mother. Only, he did not account for two men showing up. That is why Jedidiah devised a plan to see which man was right for Patience. The love seat was another one of those tests, but Jedidiah needed more time to prove that Patience and Matt were destined for each other.

"I see what you are doing, Poppy, and I want you to stop it this minute," Patience said.

Matt was still confused but interested in the conversation between Patience and Jedidiah. Jedidiah waved his hand, and the seat released them, causing Patience to spring right into Matt's arms.

"You planned that, didn't you?" She laughed as the old man put his hand over his mouth to hide his laughter. She thanked Matt for catching her in spite of the embarrassment she felt. The old man chuckled at the two who seemed more acquainted with each other than before. "I'm sorry, Matt," she said.

"I don't mind at all," he replied, still holding her in his arms. She had to remind him that it was okay to let her go. If it was up to Matt, he would have held her forever. Jedidiah was so pleased to see the interaction between them.

Something was going on in Patience's heart that had not been there before. She felt strangely happy. She was not aware that night was to become the first of many happy times over the next six months. Patience felt like Rachel from the Bible after Jacob had taken her in his arms and kissed her for the first time. Only, she was neither embraced nor kissed by Matt. That would be for another time, she hoped.

Chapter 6

FALLING IN LOVE

Matt had the same growing feelings inside him as Patience and had every intention of telling her as soon as he figured out how. They enjoyed each other on walks as their conversations deepened their friendship. Each walk became longer, and their conversations became more intimate.

One day, Matt invited Patience to walk with him to the garden because he wanted to tell her more about who he was and why he came to see her grandfather. He felt he had not been completely honest with her. He felt she deserved to know everything about him if he was going to pursue her.

He never liked conflict. Nevertheless, he knew it was inevitable if he hoped to build a relationship with her. His father had told him once that every relationship, regardless of what kind, would eventually have conflict. He also told him that conflict was not all bad. It was just a way of addressing differences of opinions with the understanding that his was not the only valid viewpoint. Matt had strong feelings for Patience and knew the only way their friendship could grow was to have the right soil to grow in. For him, the "right soil" was absolute truth.

When they arrived at the garden, it was beautiful. There was a grand fountain with an array of statues all around. A cluster of three large lions—black, white, and gold—were facing each other. They each had a pair of magnificent, falcon-like wings that stretched out, allowing the tips to touch. Under each lion's foot laid a predator with a lion's claws on its head. On one side, there were three magnificent unicorns with riders. In the middle, there were angels with trumpets to their mouths as if ready to sound the charge.

Flowers were everywhere, and the mixture of fragrances filled the air with sweet perfume. Matt took her hand and led her to the nearby bench where they both sat down. Patience could sense an uneasiness in Matt and did not know how to make him comfortable. She remained quiet with her hand in his, looking straight into his eyes, sweetly smiling. Her beautiful smile was all Matt needed to gain confidence to speak his heart. He told her all about why he and Jackson had come to see her grandfather. How famine had stripped their land of food and provisions. How his father was unable to work due to a terrible accident and that coming to see her grandfather was his last chance for help. Matt hung his head, a little ashamed of having to beg for help. However, he knew in his heart there was no shame in providing sustenance for his family.

Patience squeezed his hand, still quiet as to not interrupt. She thought it was brave of him to ask for help despite the spirit of pride. Pride was a demon spirit that kept men in the bondage of self-centeredness. It pleased her that Matt had conquered it.

After Matt explained his entire circumstances for being there, it moved Patience to compassion. She placed her other hand on top of his, assuring him she understood. How wonderful it was to find a man of honor who cared enough to express his feelings at the risk of embarrassment. That day, they talked, laughed, and held hands for what seemed like hours. It was the day love pulled them into each other's arms. Matt holding Patience in his arms made them realize that their two hearts were becoming one.

They were not the only ones who noticed their growing affection. Nothing escaped Jedidiah. He was very pleased with the couple and prayed that God's purpose would be realized in their lives.

*****

The courtship between Matt and Patience grew rapidly. At the end of the six months, Jedidiah called Matt into his inner court and asked him about his intention concerning Patience. Of course, he was well aware of Matt's love for his granddaughter. Nevertheless, he had to play the part of her father because Steven was not yet there.

"I intend to marry her, Sir," Matt said with a half-smile, unsure if what he said was acceptable. "That is, of course, with your permission," he said nervously.

Jedidiah laughed teasingly. "I know, Son. I just had to ask in a way of formality and in accordance with our customs." The old man noticed the relief in Matt's face when he told him that he should breathe. Matt laughed, unaware that he wasn't breathing. "I must tell you, Matt, that it would please me very much to see you two together. Nonetheless, it is not left to me to make that decision. I must talk with Patience's father and mother. If they feel the same as I do, there shouldn't be a problem. However, Patience is a very special young woman. She has been even as a child. God marked her in a way that is uncommon to humankind. If it is the will of the Lord for you two to be together, you will be. There is no reason to despair or worry, for I know that both of you desire only His perfect will for your lives."

Matt didn't know what to say. He just stood there, feeling like he had been punched in the stomach. Jedidiah seemed calm and unworried. Matt was worried. Tiny beads of sweat broke out on his forehead. This girl was his dream, his hope. Now, it seemed there was the possibility of them not being together. The thought of not being with her left him void. He had no idea what he was going to tell Patience or how she would react when he told her that their marriage was contingent on the approval of her parents. As in a dream, words from the past penetrated Matt's mind. It was a verse he had learned from the Holy Book: TRUST IN THE LORD WITH ALL YOUR HEART AND DO NOT RELY ON YOUR OWN UNDERSTANDING, ACKNOWLEDGE HIM IN ALL YOUR WAYS AND HE WILL DIRECT YOUR WAY. Breathing calmly, Matt held his peace and listened to the rest of what Jedidiah had to say.

Suddenly, a light thud to Matt's head from the old man's staff brought him out of his thoughts. "Ouch! What was that for?" Matt protested.

"Pay attention, and stop daydreaming, or I'll have to apply more force next time."

Matt stared at the old man, ready to hear whatever he had to say. Jedidiah cleared his throat. He looked at Matt with seriousness in his eyes. "Come with me to the sun room. Curiosity grabbed Matt's mind like it always did when something mysterious was afoot. The last time he had visited the sun room, Jackson was trying desperately to escape the claws of a gigantic cat. Matt had no desire to encounter such a beast.

Despite what was going on in Matt's mind, Jedidiah continued his quest. "There is also still the matter of the treasure," said Jedidiah. "As you know, those who come here have an opportunity to take a treasure with them when they leave. Both you and Jackson had this opportunity presented to you when you first arrived. Jackson squandered his opportunity by his self-centered behavior. You, on the other hand, revealed a character of honor and selflessness. You have become very special to me, and I want to offer you a treasure and a jewel of your choice, even the Sun Stone if it is your desire. Choose wisely, my Son, for you can only have one jewel."

Matt was puzzled by the offer but did not wish to embarrass the old man. He pondered over the decision, hoping he would make the right choice. He knew the Sun Stone meant a great deal to the old man and that the jewels were very costly. Matt thought about the treasure box. It wasn't very large, and therefore, couldn't hold a very great treasure—at least, that was his reasoning. The old man had been kind and generous to him. He felt that taking anything other than what he had already received would be a sign of ingratitude. Instead of choosing a gift, he declined to take anything.

"Oh, but you cannot decline, my Son. You must pick one of the gifts. That is the way this works," said Jedidiah.

After considering the gifts before him, Matt decided to take the box. The box was an antique. In Matt's eyes, it showed very little value on the outside. *Maybe its contents would prove just as meager*, he thought. With reluctance, Matt pointed to the box, and Jedidiah moved quickly to take it from under the Sun Stone and place it gently into the hands of the man he had come to love as a son. Matt paused briefly to turn the box around, up, and over, observing the signs and symbols on the box that looked like writing. He looked at Jedidiah who was standing in front of him smiling, and he then decided to open it.

Upon opening the box, to Matt's astonishing surprise, the greatest treasure he had ever seen was in it. He pulled it out and stared at it with tears in his eyes.

"Well, how do you like it, Matt? Is it not everything your heart has desired?"

"Yes, it is… and more," Matt said, still looking at the two objects. One was in his hand, and the other was still in the box.

"This was your last test, with the exception of Patience's parents, to see if you and my granddaughter were meant for each other. Now, without a doubt, you and I both know. I have watched the two of you over the past few months, and you have something between you that I rarely see."

Matt stood, waiting for the old man to explain what he meant.

"Others-centeredness," Jedidiah said with a smile. "You both put the other before yourself, and the wonder of it all is that you do the same for others. From what I have observed, you were made for each other. You are very like-minded, and you know a couple can't really be happy unless they are like-minded."

Jedidiah cleared his throat again, crossed his arms, and then bluntly asked Matt if he had asked Patience to marry him. Matt gave him a sheepish look. "You haven't asked her?"

"No, Sir. But…"

"Well, what are you waiting for considering you now know your destiny?"

"What about her parents?"

"What about them?" Jedidiah replied.

"What do you know in your heart, Matt?" Indeed, Matt did know in his heart that his destiny was to be with Patience.

Matt held a beautiful picture of Patience in a wedding garment in one hand and a diamond wedding ring of many colors was still in the box. He knew this was a day to be happy. Jedidiah was becoming somewhat impatient with how slowly Matt was taking the whole thing.

"This was my granddaughter's time with me, and now, that time has come to an end. While you were training for things you do not yet understand, she also was training in spiritual gifts and faith with me. She has reached her third stage and will soon depart. Your last six months are complete as well, and I am very proud of all that you have accomplished both in provision for others and in receiving a bride for yourself," exclaimed Jedidiah.

Matt was speechless. Thoughts of courtship, proposal, and marriage were swirling in his mind. One moment, he was planting seeds in a field, a seemingly simple task. Now, he was contemplating being the husband of Jedidiah's granddaughter. "This is all moving so fast. I can't keep up!" Matt nervously whispered under his breath.

The old man just laughed as he explained to Matt the impact he had made on everyone in the kingdom. "You have no idea how much food you have provided for the villages by the care you gave to the fields. Even the fields that Jackson corrupted with his greed and selfish ambition were corrected."

Fields and crops were that last things on Matt's mind. He wanted to hear more about Patience and what the old man meant by her training and departure. Was she leaving? Would she return? What about her parents? Would he finally get to meet her father? All these questions were going through Matt's mind while Jedidiah kept on with his praise about how well Matt had kept the fields.

"Never have I seen such an abundance of food during famine time," said Jedidiah. "Why... we even had plants grow up that weren't in our seed box," he said with a chuckle. "The Lord is pleased with you, Son. This means that all the families will have enough food to last through this season of great need. Well done, Son."

"It was not me, Master Jedidiah. You know as I do that it was the Lord."

The old man was glad to hear Matt give honor to the Lord. A lesser man would have taken credit for all the work. Matt was different. He understood that giving credit to whom credit was due and respecting God was bigger than any personal praise.

Jedidiah decided to share with Matt his observations of how well he had done over the past year. He took Matt outside to the bench under the tree where they both sat down. "Matt, you have been very helpful to me this past year, and I am proud of how you never grumbled, protested, or complained about anything."

Matt shifted his weight on the bench, uneasy about hearing such compliments from a man of Jedidiah's prominence.

Jedidiah continued. "I know how much you missed your family. All I can say is that God's will always comes before ours." Matt dropped his head, studying the ground around him, seemingly trying to take his mind off of his parents. He hadn't seen them in a year. He missed them desperately.

Studying Matt's face closely, Jedidiah sensed he was sensitive about the matter. The old man's compassion for him was evident. Placing his arm around Matt's shoulder, he was reassured that the old Seer understood what he was going through.

"During your stay here, you only sought to care for others. You have a strength deep inside you that I have only seen in a few. You have learned many things, my Son, and there are many more things you must master before you can fully engage the enemy."

"Enemy? What enemy?" Matt asked, puzzled by Jedidiah's words.

The old seer couldn't help but chuckle seeing the look on Matt's face. "No need to be concerned, Matt. The power to conquer is already in you."

Matt ran his fingers through his hair, feeling unsure about what Jedidiah was talking about. "Would you mind explaining exactly what you are talking about, Sir? You first mentioned enemies... then power?"

Jedidiah raised an eyebrow. "Son, you have been training for more than just planting fields and providing food. You have been training to be what God has called every man to be." Shifting from side to side and raking both hands through his hair, Matt stood, waiting for the old man's explanation. Jedidiah held out his staff for Matt to take hold of as he continued to explain.

"Why am I holding onto your staff, Master?" Matt asked.

"Because it will open your mind to what I am telling you, and you will not have so many questions."

Matt smiled as he took a firmer grip of the staff as Jedidiah continued to explain. "Matt, if you remember, some time ago, I told you that every man is called to be the Priest, Prophet, Provider, and Protector of his family. Now that you are contemplating marriage, you must be proficient in every area. The first lesson was one you have learned well, my Son. Never take credit or glory for yourself. Let others praise you as you praise God. All glory and honor goes to the Lord. Remember that, and you will grow in wisdom. You'll get your reward when the time is right, and no one will be able to take it from you. Now, follow me," said Jedidiah.

Matt was amazed by how fast things were transpiring. Wasn't he the one who complained about time moving too slowly? He declared to himself that he'd never say that again.

Suddenly, Jedidiah swung his staff to thump Matt on the head, but this time, Matt ducked and smiled at the old man with a sense of accomplishment. "Just checking to see if you are you with me," the old seer said, chuckling as they continued to walk.

"Yes, Sir. I'm here ready to go."

Jedidiah laughed and told Matt to follow him.

"Where are we going, Sir?"

"To a place of honor, Son... to a place of honor," expressed the old man, walking ahead as Matt caught up to him. Then, they entered the Great Hall.

Walking along the corridor, suddenly, Jedidiah stopped at a small wooden door. The door was odd in that it did not look like any of the doors or woodwork inside the mansion. It matched the outside of the tree more than the inside décor. Observing the door intently, Matt thought it was odd and out of place. Jedidiah stood back as Matt continued to study the door. As Matt turned to look at the old seer for an explanation, wooden hands emerged from the door and took hold of Matt. Astonished by what was going on, Matt quickly braced himself to keep from being pulled into the door. All the strength he had gained from working in the fields seemed useless and no match for the hands that gripped him. Matt turned to his master for help, but the old man stood his distance as Matt struggled to get loose. "I can use some help here, Sir!" Matt yelled.

But Jedidiah simply stared at Matt as the hands pulled him inside. After Matt was inside, Jedidiah stepped forward and knocked on the door. "Are you in there, Matt?" he called.

"Yes, I'm in here," he yelled back, still gripped by the wooden hands.

Laughing to himself, Jedidiah walked closer to the door when another set of wooden hands grabbed him and drew him into the door.

"Sir? My Lord? Where are you?" Matt could hardly move, and his eyes were closed shut by an unknown force. Fear seemed to strike his heart as he was unable to control his movements. Calling out louder, he called on Jedidiah once more.

This time, the seer answered, "Matt, relax... Open your eyes."

"I... can't... I'm trying..." A peculiar sound could be heard at a long distance. It sounded like footsteps, but a weird, clattering sound followed. "What's that sound?" An expected answer from Jedidiah was only met with silence. Panic seemed to cripple his thoughts, and he was unsure of what to do. The footsteps seemed to move faster, and the clattering sound became more intense, moving closer and closer toward Matt. Sweat beads broke out on his face. Never had he felt so helpless and insecure. "Where are you? Why aren't you answering me?"

Abruptly, the footsteps stopped, almost seeming to understand Matt's words. Matt held his breath, hoping the sound would go away. As he seemed to calm down, the footsteps began again, but this time, they were louder and came more swiftly toward him. It was trotting… now running… now just a few yards from him. "Help me, Master! Help!" Still nothing. "Okay, what am I going to do? This is either a test, or I'm going to encounter some unknown being. Either way, I could die."

He then reminded himself of what Jedidiah said when they first entered the wooden door: "Relax. Open your eyes." Breathing in deeply, Matt calmed his heart and mind. He encouraged himself by saying, "You can do this, Matt. Now, believe! Will yourself to open your eyes."

As soon as he spoke the words, a bright, illuminous light filled the room. Matt was released and found himself standing next to the old seer. Except for the light in front of them, the rest of the room was still dark. Looking toward Jedidiah, he said, "The light is very bright, yet the room is not filled with its light. Why does the darkness remain?"

"Light is the absence of darkness," explained Jedidiah. "But in the human heart, even where God lives, there is still the propensity for us to fall into darkness."

"Then, how do we rid ourselves of this darkness?" Matt asked. It comes by prayer and faith, Matt. Prayer and faith." Then, with the raising of his staff, the entire room was filled with light.

The anxiety Matt once felt was gone. In an instant, they found themselves on the outside of the door. Matt had learned a valuable lesson. Not everything he would face would be of this world.

Walking toward Matt, Jedidiah said, "There will be times, Matt, when you can't depend on others to help you. In those times, you must use your faith."

The old man's words left Matt in deep thought. Would he ever be ready for the work ahead of him? This time, Jedidiah patted Matt on the back and proceeded toward their destination.

Chapter 7

TESTING

Continuing down the long corridor, they approached the center of the hall. The natural shine from the walls became brilliant.

Matt was very cautious after his encounter with the wooden door. "Why are the walls shimmering, and what's that light ahead coming out of that room?" Matt asked, still suspect of anything unusual.

When the old man placed his hand on the young man's shoulder, his demeanor became calm. "You will find out soon enough. Just keep in step with me until we arrive."

Matt had not seen Patience for a while, and his concern for her grew with every step he took. "Sir, I'm happy for all of this attention, but where is Patience?" He asked.

The seer said nothing. He only smiled and continued walking. Matt was agitated and wanted an answer. Resisting the impetuous impulse to act on emotions, he settled his spirit and focused on the seer.

Jedidiah was keenly aware of Matt's struggle. However, he knew that each struggle would strengthen him to perfection. "Now is not the time for questions, Matt. Keep walking. We will be there soon."

Matt's mind was working overtime, trying to figure out what Jedidiah was up to. Mumbling under his breath, he reluctantly followed Jedidiah. It seemed like time was going at a snail's pace.

Jedidiah's abrupt stop alarmed Matt. He looked in all directions, hoping to see whatever it was that caused the old man to stop. "What, Sir? What do...?" Before Matt could finish his sentence, Jedidiah held his staff out horizontally, indicating to Matt that two choices laid before him. "I don't understand, Sir. Which way are we going?"

"Not we, Matt. You," said the seer. "This fork in your path... If you listen carefully, you will hear a voice in the back of your mind telling you the way. Listen carefully because there is only one right path. Choose wisely, or it could be fatal to your future."

Before Matt could protest or ask another question, the old man vanished. "What was that?" Matt said, startled out of his mind. "How am I supposed to know which path to take when they both look the same?" In his frustration, a still, small voice came to his mind: *This is the way, Matt. Walk this way.* He didn't know whether to trust the voice or to ignore it. Jedidiah never finished his words regarding the paths. *What would he do in this situation?* Matt asked himself? The thought of being thumped on the head with the old man's staff came to mind several times before he decided to trust the voice. He moved to his right and started down the hall, hoping the voice in his head was right.

Matt walked very cautiously, looking back and forth over his shoulder. He didn't know what to expect, but whatever came, he planned to be ready. Because he was the only one traveling the path, he thought running would get him to his destination a lot faster than walking. Without wasting another minute, he took off like a gazelle. The muscles in his legs and arms were strong and vibrant. The more he ran, the more energetic he became. In no time, he had reached the door at the end of the hall. His body was not winded or tired. He felt like he could run forever. He put out his hand to take hold of the door knob, and to his surprise, the voice in his mind said, *Don't do it*. Matt was confused and frustrated. He had come this far, and he had no intention of not going through the door in front of him. A little skeptical, he readied himself to jump back in case the door or something behind the door reached for him.

Upon opening the door, he saw nothing at first. As his eyes adjusted, he could see the back of the room. Fear took hold of him. He could feel the presence of something in the room with him but could not identify what it was. Suddenly, a huge, snarling beast came out of nowhere. Matt was not able to make out its form but knew it had big teeth and long claws. It ran toward Matt who quickly closed the door, but it was to no avail. The beast broke through and leapt toward Matt, missing him barely. Matt turned and, with every muscle stretched to its limit, took off in the opposite direction. The beast ran as hard and as fast as it could to catch him but to no avail. In a matter of seconds, Matt could not be seen. The beast returned to the shattered door. As it walked through the door, the door reverted back to an unshattered state.

Matt had stopped and backtracked to see if the beast was still following. From a distance, he saw the phenomenal event of the creature going through a shattered door that reconstructed itself. He yelled at the top of his voice, "What the heck is going on?" Everything pointed to another test. *That's it. Another blasted test.* He wondered if there would be more. What was it that the old seer had said? *Don't rely on what you think you know.* Matt told himself that none of it made any sense to him, and maybe that was the point. Why would he need to go through these tests, especially the kind that could end in death?

Matt ran his fingers through his hair. Then, it finally dawned on him that he had escaped from an arm-grabbing door and had just outrun a monster beast with teeth a foot long. He started laughing out loud, not knowing if he had lost his mind or if he was just happy he was still alive. Jedidiah had told him that his training was more than just mental or physical. It was also spiritual. He finally realized that, if he didn't start using what little skills he had learned from the old man, he wouldn't be around long enough to tell Patience how much he loved her. *Concentrate,*

Matt. Stand your ground, and be courageous. You cannot run away from what you must face, or you will miss what is before you, said the voice in his head. *If I hadn't run for my life, I would have been killed or eaten by that beast,* he argued. *Running is part of being brave, Matt. Only use your running ability to outwit your foes,* said the voice.

"Am I going mad, or am I really having a conversation with a voice in my head?" Matt said.

Matt wasn't sure what to do next, so he did what he always did. He sat down for a moment to ponder before he started for the door again. He was very surprised when he was joined by two dogs the size of ordinary shepherds. The dogs were beautiful in color. Their coats were like wool. One was male. The other, female. The male weighed a few pounds more than his counterpart. Matt was not afraid but curious as to where they had come from. The dogs had webbed feet with claws and fangs that hung out the sides of their mouth like sabers. Their tails were long and fanned out at the end like fish fins when they wagged them. Matt didn't know what to think. "Well, I guess if you were going to eat me, you would have done it by now," he said to the dogs. The dogs understood and nuzzled up next to him, licking his face. "Stranger things have happened around here today, but you are a welcomed relief," he said while rubbing them.

Suddenly, the big male stood and began to growl. Joined by his mate, they both stood in front of Matt in a protected stance.

"What is it? What's going on?" Matt blurted out as if he was talking to humans.

It wasn't long before he saw what disturbed the dogs. It was the same beast he had run away from just moments ago. Only this time, there were two, and they did not look friendly.

"Let's go!" he commanded the dogs, but they stood in place. "Didn't you hear me? Let's go! Unless you want to become lunch for those beasts!" Still, the dogs remained immobile.

Closer and closer the beast came, snarling, growling, and readying themselves for the attack. Matt found himself unwilling to abandon such noble animals who, in such a short time, had become so loyal. "Well, if it's a fight they want, I guess the three of us will accommodate them," Matt said as he ran toward one of the beasts with nothing but the strength in his arms and power in his hands. He ran past the dogs who quickly caught up to him, and together, they headed for the oncoming battle. The first beast leapt onto Matt with full force, landing on top of him. Matt used his powerful legs and pushed the beast, continuing with it until he found himself on top. With a powerful punch, he knocked the beast's front fang out of its mouth. Stunned from the punch, the beast used its claws and hind legs to rid itself of the human. Matt somehow landed on his feet. The beast charged again, joined by the second one. Matt said a prayer and lifted his fists, the only weapons he had to do battle.

As the beasts positioned themselves to jump, they were met by Matt's strange-looking dogs. With unparalleled agility, the dogs jumped, each sinking its fangs into the necks of the beasts. The beasts immediately fell to the floor, motionless.

Matt didn't know what to think or do. It was all so strange and had happened so fast. He looked at his new companions and thanked them. He looked at the beasts before him and noticed they were not dead but appeared to be asleep. Habitually, Matt ran his fingers through his hair, amazed at everything he had been through. Unexpectedly, the hall became unusually illuminated, and Matt wondered, *What next?*

To his delight, a familiar form walked toward him, grinning from ear to ear. It was Jedidiah. Matt had never been so glad to see anyone in all his life. The light vanished as did the beasts and the dogs as Jedidiah embraced the young warrior.

"Well done, Matt. I knew you could do it," the old man said, patting Matt on the shoulder.

Matt wanted to ask a million questions, but if there was one lesson he had learned from his ordeal, it was to listen before he spoke. Standing quietly, Matt allowed Jedidiah, who still had his arm around his neck, to lead him to wherever he was going while he listened. As they walked, anxiety and tension left Matt's body, and a pleasant feeling of peace took hold of him.

"You know, Matt, I thought those beasts were going to kick your butt there for a minute," the old man said, laughing and looking at Matt's shredded clothes.

"Believe me... I thought so, too, until my friends came along," Matt said, thanking God under his breath. "I would have been dead meat if not for those two courageous dogs you sent me."

"I sent you? You think I was the one who sent them to you?"

"Well, didn't you?" Matt asked, somewhat confused.

"No, Matt. I did not send them. They came from you."

Matt was really confused. Running his fingers through his hair, he looked at Jedidiah with questions in his eyes.

"I know that you have many questions, and in time, most of them will be answered," said the old man. "For now, let's just say that you have passed every test."

Matt was too inquisitive to leave matters unresolved. He needed to have some kind of explanation... even if it was a small one. "Will you at least tell me what I just went through in the hall back there?"

The old seer smiled, knowing that, if he didn't give his young man some explanation, he would persist until it drove both of them crazy. "In a nutshell, Matt, you have been on a journey since you arrived. It was necessary to test you to show you your strengths and weaknesses. No one knows himself without test. We often boast about what we can or will do, but no one really knows until put to the test. These halls have many such tests. Each test is designed and matched with each person that enters these halls.

The two beasts were your fears, and you had to walk these particular halls to face them. The voice in your head was me. I have been given certain gifts to enable people to embrace their God-given potential. I guided you through the test, giving you directions, but I was forbidden to rescue you. When you made up your mind to go back and face the door and what was behind it, your fear dissipated, and your courage came and stood boldly by your side." The old man smiled as understanding came into Matt's mind.

"You mean the dogs that came to my aid?"

"Yes, Matt. They were your strength and courage. And wherever you go, they will follow you. And they will be as large or small as your faith."

It was a lot to grasp. Matt was exhausted just thinking about it all. He hesitated to ask, but he could not help himself. "Am I done with being tested?"

The old man grinned and rubbed Matt's head and said, "For now, my young friend. For now."

Matt smiled, shaking his head and wondering what laid ahead of him.

Chapter 8

THE TREASURE BOX

He kept in step with Jedidiah until they arrived in front of another door. Uneasiness was in Matt's stomach. He thought to himself, *Now what?* The door opened on its own. Wide-eyed, he couldn't believe his eyes. To his surprise, he saw Patience standing on a platform beautifully dressed in a jeweled wedding dress, just like in the picture in his box. Next to her was a model of herself, just a little older. At least, that was the way she looked.

On the other side of her was a tall, brawny man. There was no mistaking who he was. The two people were dressed in regal attire and smiling at Matt who stood in the door speechless. Patience's grandparents from her father's side, Peter and Mary, had taken a short retreat from their work to celebrate their granddaughter's happy occasion.

Matt was amazed at what he saw, and having Jedidiah standing by him made it even better. He leaned over and asked Jedidiah what was going on. Jedidiah could hardly hold in his laughter. The look on Matt's surprised face was more than Jedidiah could take. Only a man like Matt could be so unpresumptuous. After the loud outburst of laughter, the old man finally calmed down enough to tell Matt he was at Patience's wedding.

Matt was not amused. His heart sank to the ground, and his demeanor was the lowest ever. He could not understand why Jedidiah had a smile on his face in the midst of such a horrible situation. "Why am I at Patience's wedding? Who is she marrying?" Matt was very frustrated, and none of it was to his liking. He stared at Patience, wide-eyed and disappointed. Here was the woman he loved about to marry another man. Why would Jedidiah bring him here? How he loved her and desired her so much that his heart broke at the thought of not having her. He had thought she loved him as well, but evidently, his assumption was wrong. Did her father already have someone picked out for her? Who could the other man be? It was probably someone of royal blood and very wealthy. Matt's mind was running wild with all kind of thoughts until Jedidiah thumped him on the head with his staff.

"What is wrong with you, Matt? It's time to meet the parents of your bride!"

The words didn't register at first. He thought he heard Jedidiah say something about Patience being his bride. Could it be true, or had his hearing gone bad? Matt looked at Jedidiah, his face stunned, hands sweaty, and his voice cracking.

"My what?" he asked excitedly. "Are you fooling with me?"

At that moment, Matt jumped five feet off the floor and ran straight toward Patience. Her parents had never seen a young man so enthusiastically open about his feelings. Patience broke into laughter at the sight of Matt dressed in shredded clothing, running down to meet her. At that point, nothing on earth could have stopped him from getting to her. The joy that filled his heart had no words.

When he reached her, he stopped just in front of Patience who was presently standing between her parents. Without hesitation, he blurted out words that could not stay caged in his heart. "I love your daughter, Sir. May I please have her hand in marriage?"

Steven smiled. Matt suddenly recognized that he must look crazy, rushing in dressed in tattered attire. Steven looked at Heather with a smile as she nodded her head in approval. He then took Matt's hand and placed it on top of his daughter's hand. He said that, because Jedidiah, his father-in-law had committed Patience long ago to a God-loving man and because he had chosen Matt to be that man, he had no objections. It was the way of their faith. Heather leaned over, kissed Matt on the cheek, and welcomed him as her son.

By this time, Matt was so elated that he picked Patience up and twirled her around. He then sat her back down on her feet. He then fell to his knees and officially asked Patience to marry him. When she said, "Yes," he was elated, and the most incredible thing happened. In front of everyone, Matt's countenance was changed. He felt more strength enter his body, and his senses were enhanced. It was like an extreme makeover—only on the inside. Then, his clothes became a brilliant white, sparkling with tiny diamonds embedded in the material. Patience's dress matched Matt's wedding garment. No garment more beautiful had ever been made.

Where Matt was kneeling, to the right of his knee, was his treasure box sparkling. When he reached for it, it opened of its own accord. Inside was that beautiful, jeweled ring of many colors with a touch of Sun Stone in the center. When Matt placed it on her finger, the entire room lit up.

Behind Patience and her parents, stood his mentor and friend, Jedidiah. For the first time, Matt understood who this man really was. For an entire year, Matt had been sitting with him, working the fields, listening to his wisdom, and having the time of his life. He had laughed and enjoyed the best of everything with him, and yet it never occurred to Matt that he had been in the presence of the king and priest of the realm. Matt knelt down again to give honor to the king for the gracious hospitality and honor he had enjoyed under his tutelage.

Jedidiah, of course, could not let a good opportunity to laugh escape him, so he reached past Patience to where Matt was still kneeling and thumped him on the head and said, "Are you ready to get married, Son?" They all laughed as Matt rose and joined his young bride. As they stood in front of Jedidiah, who was now in the role of priest, they were speechless, but their eyes said everything. The joy in Jedidiah's eyes told of his delight and gratitude. How happy it made him to see his granddaughter in the arms of a man who loved her more than his own life. After Jedidiah preformed the ceremony, he had Peter and Mary, Steven's parents, come forward and lay hands on their children to bless them. When they had finished, all in the room said, "Amen."

Rising from their knees, Matt and Patience were rushed into a large room where a great celebration included music, dancing, food, drink, and hundreds of the king's people who were gathered to join the festivities. It was delightful.

The old man came up to his granddaughter and asked her, "How do you like your gift, my Dear?"

"Oh, Poppy, it's the most wonderful gift in the world! I will love him forever!"

"I think he feels the same way about you." He laughed and kissed her on the cheek.

Steven and Heather stood, watching the festivities. Heather seized the opportunity to talk with Matt, enjoying his charming demeanor and watching him watch their daughter. It was so evident how much he loved her.

At about that time, Patience took his hand and joined in the dancing celebration of their marriage. "Are you enjoying yourself, my Darling," she asked.

"Very much, my Love. The only thing missing are my parents. How I wish they were here."

"I know, Matt. I'm sorry they could not come with your father having so many responsibilities for helping people in the village. From what you told me, your parents are essential to the welfare of the entire village." She took his face in her hands and kissed him. "I'm sure they will rejoice when they see us." Matt was encouraged by his young bride. She had been healing to his heart in the absence of his family. Apart from God, she was now his reason for living.

After everyone was gone and Matt and Patience were left alone, she took his hand and led him to a room at the end of the Great Hall. As they entered the room, the door closed behind them, and the room suddenly burst into an array of colors. It was like being in the middle of a thousand rainbows. There were no flowers to be seen, but the colors gave off the aroma of freshly cut flowers. Patience could smell magnolias, roses, honeysuckles, and lavender. There was the smell of jasmine, brugmansia, lilac, and cranberry vinca all emanating from the rainbow colors that seemed to have no end.

Patience was thrilled, and when Matt swept her off her feet into his arms, she giggled and waited for the kiss she knew was coming. When he put her down, they took a tour through the room, amazed at all they saw.

"Did you know about this room?" Matt asked.

"I knew about it but not like this… Poppy did this," she said and laughed.

What a time they had, exploring the world around them and enjoying each other. What sweet, innocent love they shared. For the first time, each felt the touch of love and knew the oneness of a husband and wife. How beautiful it was to be entangled and wrapped in untarnished passion. Love had finally found them, and it was well worth the wait.

Chapter 9

CARETAKERS

I t was six more months before Matt was able to visit his parents, who Jedidiah assured had been well cared for. Matt's father had fully recovered, and life was smiling on them.

During the next six months, Matt was learning yet another lesson from his mentor. The old man was teaching him the hardest lesson of all: how to read the hearts of people. He had mastered reading maps and stars and even weather, but Jedidiah told him that the human heart was hardest of all to read because it was filled with deception and corruption beyond anything else on the face of the earth. Even when read properly, it still is ever changing. The truth, he told Matt, was that only God could really read hearts. Nevertheless, a man who loved God could get insight and revelation, especially when it suited the purpose of God. Matt understood this well and promised to use his talent for good, whatever tools and skills the Lord allowed him to have.

During those months, Jedidiah took Matt through every room in the mansion, showing him things no one else had ever seen. Matt was not aware that the tree was planted by the rivers of water and that its roots went down deeper than any tree on earth. It was the tree that was connected to the source of life, and it was filled with unexplainable wonders, cures, wealth, provisions for the poor, and insight. Wisdom and understanding was in the tree and could be obtained by a diligent and inquisitive mind.

Jedidiah said, "These things will be given freely to those who diligently seek after truth and honor. Just as you came and found your heart's desire, so there are others who will come and seek their heart's desire. Some will have the same kind of spirit as Jackson and will lose everything. Others will have a heart like yours and will aim to give rather than to receive. Still, there are others who will come to rob, steal, and even kill to gain the treasure that is hidden here. Of course, those who have such a heart will end up in the rugs of greed and torment or on the wall of despair. If you remember, you were the reason Jackson did not stay in the rug, and I must say you made a good choice, for I have watched his actions since the day he left. To my delight, his heart seems to have changed, yet my spirit senses not all is as it appears. He has cared for his mother and for your parents since he left, but the relationship between your mother and his has not been fully healed. On your visit to see them, take Jackson this gift. It will cause him to prosper because the Lord does not withhold good things from a repentant heart. However, if there is guile and deception in his heart, it will be revealed by his rejection of your gift.

"Your parents will be delighted to see you and Patience. You may stay with them for a season, but you must then return. It is the Lord's will that you work from the Great Tree to serve others when they come as you and Jackson did. You and Patience will serve together even as I have done so in the days of my youth. You and Patience will live happily in this land, and your children will prosper in every way as long as your hearts are turned to the Lord. You must remember at all times that with great gifts comes great responsibility. And with great prosperity and blessings come suffering and sorrow."

After Jedidiah had finished instructing Matt and Patience in their duties, he blessed them and sent them off to Matt's home village, Columbidae. Patience had never been outside the kingdom and was looking forward to seeing everything. She had longed to help and serve those who could not help themselves. After all, she came from a line of missionaries who gave all to win others to Jesus. Now clinging to her husband, she had an opportunity to do the same. They traveled toward Matt's home with great expectations and wagons loaded with provisions. Their desire was to love God and share with people the greatest treasure of all: God's love.

Matt and Patience could hardly wait to share their joy with his friends and family. They had experienced many wonders together, but Matt would never forget the greatest lesson he had learned from the old man: "Wherever a man's treasure is, that is where his heart will be. The greater a man loves God, the greater his treasure will be, and only a pure and humble heart can obtain life-lasting treasure from the Treasure Tree."

*"…If you call out for insight and cry aloud for under-standing, and if you look for it as for silver and search for it as for hidden **Treasure**, then you will understand the fear of the Lord and find the knowledge of God."*

—*Proverbs 2:3–5*

FAMILY DEVOTIONAL LESSONS

"Do not lay up for yourselves treasures on earth, where moth and rust consume and where thieves break in and steal, but lay up for yourselves treasures in heaven, where neither moth nor rust consumes and where thieves do not break in and steal. For where your treasure is, there will your heart be also." (Matthew 7:19-21)

In your family devotional, look up the scriptures about "treasure" and discuss how you can apply them to your everyday lives. How can you share them with your family and friends?

"God will be the sure foundation for your time, a rich store of salvation and wisdom and knowledge; the fear of the Lord is the key to this treasure." (Isaiah 33:6)

(The *fear of the Lord* means having a loving respect and reverence for God... to obey Him and those who represent Him.)

Every Christian has a treasure tree full of fruit and gifts. The box is your heart, and the gifts and fruit are found in 1 Corinthians 12:7-11 and Galatians 5:22. You must put obedience in your treasure tree in order to receive and utilize these gifts and fruit.

*"For where your **treasure** is, there your heart will be also." (Matthew 6:21)*

There is a danger in having treasure if it takes your heart from God.

Identify several of your favorite treasures (important things to you). Determine if they or God is first priority in your life. The First Commandment is to love God before other things.

*"You are the Lord's prized **treasure** He died for you; what are you willing to do for Him?" (Matthew 10:37-39)*

The daily reading of your Bible, praying for each other, and attending Church will keep your **treasures** safe.

Blessings on you,
Pastor Bruce

THIS STORY IS JUST BEGINNING!

Don't miss the exciting adventure of Matt and Patience in Book Two, *Coming Home*, as they explore a world of wonder but also evil and spiritual warfare. No one suspects anything they can't see. But often, it is what you don't see that can destroy the very thing you love. Join them as they face unseen enemies of the Realm. Witness Matt as he sees Jackson for who he is…

EXCERPT FROM BOOK TWO, *COMING HOME*…

"Stolen Treasures are of no value,
but righteousness delivers from death."
Proverbs 10:2

"There was a knock on the door of the cabin, and immediately, there was the sound of movement inside. Soon, the door opened. A wide-eyed woman in her early forties stood in the doorway with her husband, looking over her shoulder. Both of them were surprised and overjoyed. Their eyes filled with tears as they stood, staring at the young couple in their doorway. At last, their son was home. At least, he looked like their son. The young man in front of them was twice the size of the young man who left what seemed like a decade ago. Where had the time gone? One year away had turned into three years for Frances and Jeremy. Jedidiah had a way of altering elements, and time was one of them.

Frances looked in his eyes and knew without doubt that it was Matt. And with him was a woman of uncommon, exquisite beauty. Matt stood with the biggest grin on his face, and it was clear to Frances and Jeremy that the young woman belonged to him. It was now time to celebrate. Without further hesitation, Frances leapt into her son's arms and wept like a baby."

For more information, visit…

www.HighBridgeBooks.com/BruceAndVernaeEwing

CPSIA information can be obtained
at www.ICGtesting.com
Printed in the USA
FFOW03n0022151215
19495FF